*How a Weirdo
and a Ghost
Can Change
Your Entire Life*

OTHER YEARLING BOOKS YOU WILL ENJOY:

How a Weirdo and a Ghost Can Change Your Entire Life

PATRICIA WINDSOR

Illustrated by Jacqueline Rogers

A Yearling Book

Published by
Dell Publishing
a division of
The Bantam Doubleday Dell Publishing Group, Inc.
666 Fifth Avenue
New York, New York 10103

Text copyright © 1986 by Patricia Windsor
Illustrations copyright © 1986 by Jacqueline Rogers

The trademark Yearling® is registered in the U.S. Patent
and Trademark Office.

ISBN: 0-440-40094-5

Reprinted by arrangement with Delacorte Press

Printed in the United States of America

August 1988

10 9 8 7 6 5 4

CW

To My Children

*How a Weirdo
and a Ghost
Can Change
Your Entire Life*

1.

Martha had a strep throat the whole winter. At least, that's how it seemed, like forever, even though her mother said it was only two weeks. Her head ached, her throat felt like a furry sock, and her tongue looked like a lizard. She felt like a dead body and was glad her mom kept poking her to see if she was still alive.

The whole family tried to cheer her up. Dad told his worst jokes, and Mom baked chocolate chip cookies even though she was against sweets. Jemima, Martha's older sister, bought her a giant box of Crayolas. The trouble was, all the blues looked like milk of magnesia and all the pinks like Pepto-Bismol. Everyone tried real hard, but nothing made Martha feel any better.

"Here's a card from Jenny," Mom said one morning. "That should pep you up."

Martha looked at the picture of a grinning rabbit and didn't feel any peppier. When she read the note Jenny had written inside, she felt worse.

Dear Martha,
The news is this. I am best friends with Phyllis Blott from now on. I hope you don't get mad but if you do, get well soon anyway.

The stinking rats, Martha thought. She and Jenny had promised to be best friends forever. They'd made a secret pact to always be faithful and true and never be best friends with anyone else.

Who cares, Martha told herself. She was too busy being sick to get mad. She was positive she would be sick for years.

But one morning she woke up and everything smelled different. All kinds of smells came with the morning: car fumes, coffee, Dad's after-shave, and the strawberry mousse Jemima gunked on her hair. Ever since the strep throat these smells had made Martha feel like throwing up. All of a sudden she felt hungry enough to eat a horse. When her mother brought in a bowl of gloppy gray oatmeal, Martha gobbled it up in a split second.

"I see you're feeling better!" her mom exclaimed. "It's time we did something about your homework."

Martha groaned. She pulled the sheet over her head. "I think I'm still sick," she said.

Her mother didn't believe her. "I'll call the school and see if Jenny can bring your work home. Then you two can have a visit."

"Not her," Martha said. "I'm not friends with Jenny anymore."

"Oh?" Mom asked, pulling the sheet down to Martha's chin. "When did you decide that?"

"I didn't decide," Martha said. "She'd rather be best friends with Phyllis Blott."

"What nonsense," Mom said, fluffing up the pillows. "I'm sure all three of you can be friends."

"Phyllis Blott has teeth like a vampire. Two big long

ones that stick out over her lip." Martha demonstrated, but her mother was unimpressed.

"It doesn't matter what people look like, Martha dear."

"She also has a pool, two cats, and a dog, which is probably why Jenny likes her better than me."

"I'm sure that's not true," Mom said.

But Martha knew it was. Jenny loved to swim, and she was always wishing she could have a pet. They didn't allow pets in the Grape Hill Apartments where Martha and Jenny lived. And there was only the big public pool to swim in. It got crowded with all the little kids trying to slam-dunk you. Phyllis Blott lived in a private house in Melody Woods. She was probably rich.

It was very unfair, Martha thought. If you're best friends with someone, you should like them even if they don't have a pool, two cats, and a dog. You should like them for what they are.

"Don't worry about it too much," Mom said. "Things will get back to normal when you go back to school. Jenny's a nice girl."

"She is not," Martha said. "She cheats on tests and she doesn't understand half the stuff I tell her."

But Mom wasn't really listening. She opened the curtains, pulled up the shade, and picked up the breakfast tray. She said she would go for her run, since Martha was feeling better.

"I'm still hungry!" Martha said.

"I'll make you a nice spinach omelet for lunch," Mom said.

Martha's mother was a health nut, which was why she was against sweets and for vegetables. The smell of bacon was coming from the apartment downstairs where Mr. and Mrs. Morris lived with their son, Archie. Mrs. Morris never worried about cholesterol or gaining weight. If Martha got a craving for a junk food snack, she went down to Mrs. Morris who always had bags of nacho chips and jelly doughnuts. She felt like sneaking down there while her mother was out for a jog.

But instead she stayed in bed and thought about Jenny and Phyllis Blott. Jenny wasn't so great to have as a friend anyway. Martha had this neat book about Venice that she had bought at a yard sale for a quarter. It explained how Venice had canals instead of streets and how people used boats called gondolas to get around. When Martha told this to Jenny, Jenny thought she was describing some new TV miniseries. And when Martha said "wouldn't it be fun to get to school in a gondola instead of a school bus?" Jenny wrinkled her nose and got Tessa Murphy and Diane Fink to laugh with her. "Who wants to get seasick riding to school on a slimy old canal?" they'd said, and cracked up in the lunchroom. Martha had felt really disappointed. What were friends for if they couldn't pretend to be interested in the same things you were?

All of a sudden Martha's brain clicked with an idea. If you didn't have any friends in the first place, they couldn't disappoint you, could they? And if you didn't have a best friend, you wouldn't have to worry about getting get-well cards full of bad news.

Okay, Martha thought, no more friends. She could talk to the kids in school, but she wouldn't be friends.

As soon as she decided this she felt a lot better. And

she felt sleepy. She drifted off, dreaming about bacon and eggs.

Then she woke up again with a horrible thought. It was going to be embarrassing to go back to school with everyone knowing about Jenny and her. They'd probably feel sorry for her, or laugh, or think she was a loser.

It was double lousy to have to put up with strep throat and Phyllis Blott at the same time. Martha wished she could hop a gondola and run away to Venice.

2.

Martha ate the spinach omelet for lunch and it wasn't so bad. Food tasted like a new and unusual thing. Now that she was feeling better, she was also feeling bored. She decided to read her Venice book, which she hadn't been able to do for so long because the fever made the words jump around in front of her eyes. Before she opened it, she held the green book in her hands and felt the soft cloth binding. Then she smelled it. A little of the nice smell of old dry autumn leaves was there, but not as much as when she'd bought it.

She was busy counting the number of palaces along the Grand Canal, which was like Venice's main street, when Mom announced that Teddy Winterrab was at the door.

"What for?" Martha shrieked in alarm.

Teddy Winterrab was weird. Nobody liked him. He looked weird, acted weird, and talked weird. Everybody called him Teddy Windbag because he talked so much.

"He brought your homework," Mom said.

"Tell him I'm contagious," Martha said. "Don't let him in!"

But Mom just laughed. "Put on your robe and let me

run a comb through your hair. Then I'll tell him to come in. He says he's got to explain some of the work to you."

"I don't need any hair comb for him," Martha grumbled, but she put on her robe and made sure she buttoned it right up to her chin. She didn't want Teddy seeing her panda pajamas.

Teddy stood in her bedroom doorway, holding a big black briefcase.

"Hello," Martha said in a weak, sickly voice. She hoped he would be scared off by germs. But he came straight across the room to her bed, and for a horrible moment it looked like he might sit on the bed next to her. But he dragged over the chair from her desk, sat down and put the briefcase on his lap. Martha let her eyelids droop. She had never seen him up close before, and she didn't want him to notice her staring. His blond hair was fuzzy and his ears were pointy and one of his front teeth was chipped. He opened his briefcase with a loud *thwuck*.

"I have here your math and your history," Teddy said in an official way. "There's a quiz next week on chapter five. And here's the list of spelling words. There's a test on them too."

Martha stared at the list of words. There were multitudes. They jumped around in front of her eyes. Teddy's voice droned on. He sounded just like the school principal. Martha sat up.

"So, is this all?" she asked. "Are you sure you brought me enough?"

Teddy stopped busily shuffling papers and looked at her. Behind his glasses, his eyes were brown, and he had beautiful long eyelashes. But they were funny eyes, shifty and weird.

"It's not my fault," he snapped. "I'm only the messenger."

He slapped the sheaf of papers down on the bed. "Besides, I have to do the same stupid work myself, don't forget!"

Martha jumped as the papers smacked her leg. "Okay, okay," she said, feeling a little bad for taking it out on him. If she cooperated, he would leave in a minute. He gave her the creeps. Look at his fingernails. They were filthy. Fingernails like that shouldn't be allowed in the room of a sick person.

"Just tell me what I have to do."

Teddy explained the history assignment. "Mrs. Gold wants us to do a project. We have to be creative. We have to think of an original way to depict Colonial life." He was talking along like a robot when suddenly he stopped. He flung the history Ditto down with the other papers, stuck out his tongue and blew a big raspberry through his pudgy lips.

Martha wanted to laugh but she wasn't sure. It was Teddy Windbag, and you had to be careful. She pretended to be busy scribbling down his instructions.

"Did you get all that?" he asked.

Martha nodded and kept her head down, trying not to smile.

"Good. Then I'm finished." He banged down the lid of the briefcase and stood up.

"Wait a minute." Martha spoke without thinking. Having someone to talk to had cheered her up, even if that someone was Teddy Winterrab. And there were some things she wanted to know. Like were Jenny and Phyllis bragging about being friends?

17

"You don't have to go right away," Martha said. "You can stay a minute, can't you?"

"What for?" Teddy asked.

Martha was startled. "Well, in the first place it's rude to just walk out on a sick person. You're supposed to say things to cheer them up."

He seemed to ponder this. He sat down again. "I guess homework assignments aren't very cheerful," he said. "I guess they make you feel sicker."

"You can say that again."

"What's the second place?"

"Huh?" Martha said.

"You said in the first place it's rude to walk out on a sick person. If you do that, you also have to say what's in the second place. Otherwise it's bad grammar."

"I was wrong," Martha said. "Don't stay. Correcting a sick person's grammar is as bad as giving them homework."

"Sorry," Teddy said, but he didn't make a move to leave. Instead he began picking things up from her night table and inspecting them. He opened the giant box of Crayolas.

"All the tops are broken," he said.

"Only the blues and pinks," Martha said. "I had a fit and bit their heads off."

Teddy looked wary. "I thought you had strep," he said. "I was the only one who volunteered to come. Nobody else would, not even Mrs. Gold. I'm very healthy, I never catch things. And anyway, I got out of school early."

Boy, Martha thought. Now she knew how lepers felt. "I did have a strep throat," she said to Teddy. She was glad that she had decided against having friends. They were good for nothing.

"It must be boring lying in bed all day," Teddy said. "When you have to get up every morning to go to school, you wish you could stay in bed forever. But it's not so much fun when you get to do it."

Martha was amazed that Teddy understood what she was feeling. "That's the truth," she said. She smiled a little.

He smiled back, showing his broken tooth. "So what do you do all day, besides eat crayons?"

"Nothing much." But the truth was, she suddenly felt like telling him about Jenny and Phyllis Blott. She almost had to bite her tongue to keep from spouting off like a faucet. For all she knew, he would go back and tell everybody what she said, and they'd all have a good laugh.

She watched as he poked through her stuff. He had finished with the night table and was now rummaging through the books strewn on her bed. It was some kind of nervous habit, Martha decided. He pulled out the little green book. "What's this?" he asked, idly turning the cover.

"Nothing!" Martha cried, and grabbed the book away from him.

Teddy stood up. "I'm going," he said.

She could tell his feelings were hurt. But she couldn't stop herself from saying "So go!" in a nasty voice. What was she doing having a conversation with Teddy Windbag anyway?

His shoulders looked all humpy and sad as he walked to the door.

"Hey, listen," she said. "I'm sorry."

He did not turn around.

"Hey! I said I was sorry!"

He stopped.

"It's just that you wouldn't understand," she said. "About the book, I mean."

He turned around and looked at her. "How do you know?" he asked.

"I just know, that's all," Martha said, thinking about Jenny and Tess and Diane laughing.

"Try me," Teddy said. "What's the big mystery anyhow?"

Before she knew it, he had come back and plopped down in the chair again. Martha silently handed him the book. He took it, opened it up and leafed through the pages, chewing on his bottom lip.

Martha couldn't tell anything from his expression. Finally he murmured, "Hey, this is a real old book. It has a map too. Wow."

Martha just gaped at him in astonishment.

"You know, this place Venice, it's a haunty sort of place," he said, and handed the book back. "Great authors have written stories about it." Teddy's shifty eyes looked wistful. "I sure would like to go there."

"You would?"

Questions and ideas and things to talk about came tumbling through Martha's mind. She didn't know where to start. But she never got a chance because her mother appeared at the door.

"I think that's enough for a first visitor," she said. "It was nice of you to bring Martha's homework, Ted."

Teddy's face closed up, and his eyes got shifty and

weird again. He doesn't trust grown-ups, Martha thought.

Teddy followed Martha's mother out of the bedroom. He had left his black briefcase on the floor next to the chair. Martha felt sure he planned it, because in a moment he was back. He came up to the bed, leaned over, and whispered in her ear: "Did you ever try a Ouija board?"

Martha shrank back a little. "A what?"

"It's just like Venice. Haunty."

"Where are you, Ted?" Martha's mother called out in a worried voice.

"I'll bring it next time," Teddy whispered. "I'm coming, Mrs. Lewis," he shouted.

When he was gone, Martha lay in her bed thinking for a long time. People, she decided, aren't at all like what you think they are. You could get it all wrong. Like thinking Jenny would always be her best friend. Like thinking Teddy Winterrab was weird.

Well, actually, Teddy *was* weird. But in a more interesting way than Martha had imagined.

She couldn't help wondering when "next time" would be. It was amazing, but she could hardly wait.

3.

The next morning there was more noise than usual in the bathroom. Jemima was shouting over her hair dryer.

"Mellow Rollings is a creep! Get rid of him!"

"But what will I tell him, dear?" Mom asked.

"Tell him to get lost!" Jemima cried, and slammed the bathroom door.

Later Martha found out that Mellow Rollings, a boy in Jemima's class, had stopped by to walk her to school. Jemima would have been ecstatic if Larry Haggerty had wanted to walk her to school. She had a crush on him and talked about him all the time to her friend Denise. "Larry scratched his ear in biology today," she once said. "Lawrence A. Haggerty is *the* only reality."

But instead of Larry Haggerty this Mellow Rollings person had arrived. Mom thought it was nice. "But Jemima sneaked out through the laundry room," she told Martha when she came in with another bowl of gloppy oatmeal. "Poor Mellow was still waiting in the lobby when Mrs. Morris went down for the mail. It was way past time for school."

Mellow Rollings might or might not be a creep, Martha thought, but he sure was stupid.

"I think you can get up a little today," Mom said.

Martha put on her robe and walked to the living room, feeling wobbly. She looked around the room, and everything seemed new and unfamiliar, as if she had been away a long time.

"I'm going for my jog," Mom said as she dumped a pile of books in Martha's lap. "You'll want to get back to work on this."

Martha hadn't done any homework at all last night. Instead she had been busy looking up *Ouija board* in the dictionary. She had tried *weeja*, but that didn't get anywhere. What good was a dictionary when you didn't know how to spell the word in the first place? Finally she had to ask Jemima. It was risky to do that because you never knew how Jemima would react. She could either tell you the answer or scream "Moooommmm! Guess what Martha wants to know!"

"O-U-I-J-A," Jemima had said without even looking up from the bed where she was cutting out holes in one of her sweatshirts. Martha had hurried back to bed, her legs feeling like Jell-O. It was amazing, but Jemima did have a brain even if sometimes she acted like she didn't know her own name—usually when she was mooning about Larry Haggerty, the only reality.

The dictionary said the Ouija board could be used to receive messages from the spirit world. You used a planchette to spell out the words. Martha had to look up *planchette*, which turned out to be a small board with a pencil that did automatic writing. The whole thing sounded just like the kind of weird thing a weird person like Teddy Winterrab would do. The dictionary didn't say if it was real or not either. Martha looked out the living room window and wondered what Jenny would think. They would have a laugh about Teddy and his crazy ideas.

Then she remembered. She wouldn't be telling Jenny anything anymore. Jenny could walk right past Martha's building, number 1804, and Martha wouldn't pay any attention. Jenny wouldn't stop and sit on the steps. And they wouldn't bike down Grape Hill anymore or stop and throw stones in the duck pond that was always covered with fuzzy green guck. When a stone went in, the pond went *slurp* like a monster. They used to scare little kids on Halloween by telling them a monster lived in the pond, and sometimes the kids cried and ran away while she and Jenny laughed.

That was a stupid, mean thing to do to little kids, Martha thought. Jenny's idea too. I'm not doing any dumb things like that anymore.

She opened her history book and started doing her homework.

Mom came back all sweaty from jogging. She took a shower and made Martha go back to bed for lunch. Lunch was a grilled cheese sandwich with sprouts. Martha ate all around the edge of the sandwich until it looked like a cat. The sprouts made good whiskers. After that she felt tired, and Mom told her to take a nap. Martha didn't wake up until afternoon.

"Martha?" her mom was saying. "Ted is here. I guess he has more homework for you."

For a moment Martha felt annoyed. Homework, homework! Didn't they know she was sick? Then she remembered the Ouija board and rubbed the sleep out of her eyes.

Teddy tottered in the doorway. Instead of the black briefcase, he was carrying a paper bag.

"What are you waiting for?" Martha said, suddenly feeling grumpy. Somehow, seeing him in person was not the same as thinking about it. His hair looked fuzzier. She wasn't sure she wanted to be friendly.

He must have noticed because he hesitated. His fingers curled tightly around the paper bag, and this made Martha thaw a little. They looked pathetic, those fingers. She guessed he was all nervous and didn't want to show it.

"Come in," Martha said in a nicer voice.

Teddy gave one of his shifty smiles. "I brought it," he said in a whispery voice.

Martha didn't want him to know she remembered. "What?" she asked.

"Here." He put the paper bag on her knees. She reached inside and pulled out a plastic-coated board. Although it had strange pictures of the sun and moon on it, it looked just like any old board game. The alphabet was printed across the top, and there was a row of numbers underneath and the word *Good-bye* at the bottom. Martha was disappointed.

She looked in the bag and found the little triangular piece of plastic that would be the planchette. She used the correct name for it, but Teddy didn't seem to notice. He drew up a chair. Then he looked around.

"Maybe we should close the curtains so it will be dark. You get the best results when it's dark."

Martha wondered what her mother would think if she found them in a dark room pushing a piece of plastic around on a board.

25

"Leave the curtains open," she said.

"Well, okay." Teddy seemed only mildly concerned. Then he took a big breath and started talking in his official voice again.

"Now," he said. "Who do you know who's dead?"

"Huh?" Martha asked.

"It has to be a dead person," Teddy explained. "We try to get in contact with them. If they want to talk to you, they use the pusher to spell out the words on the board."

"It's called a planchette," Martha said.

"Whatever. So, who do you want to contact?"

"I don't know," Martha said. She hadn't thought of this part. Who was dead? Who was dead that she'd want to talk to? She guessed it had to be someone ordinary. John F. Kennedy was probably too busy to talk to her.

Mom's aunt Helen had died last month. Aunt Helen had been an old lady who talked through her nose. Martha didn't think it would be interesting to get any messages from her. But, of course, there was Grandpa.

"My grandfather," she said to Teddy.

"Good." He put his fingers on the planchette and told Martha to concentrate. "Here's how you do it," he said. "You let yourself go into a trance. Don't hold the pusher too tight and don't think about anything. Make your mind go blank." Teddy demonstrated how the planchette would move around, pointing from letter to letter. "You try," he directed. "And I'll write down the letters it points to."

Martha closed her eyes. She thought about her grandfather. She thought how he had always smelled of cigars and something spicy. He'd always brought her the best presents on her birthday, grown-up things, like leather gloves and a symphony by Mozart.

Nothing happened to the planchette. It stayed on the board and didn't move. Martha realized her mind was not blank.

She opened her eyes. "How can you think of a dead person and not think of anything at the same time?"

Teddy looked stumped. "It's supposed to work," he said. "Maybe you should try calling out your grandfather's name."

Martha imagined herself yelling "Grandpa!" and felt stupid.

"Listen," she said. "Have you ever done this before?"

Teddy shifted in the chair. "Sure, plenty of times."

Martha glared at him.

"Well," he admitted, "I tried it."

"Did it work?"

Teddy looked down at his knees and began picking at the bedspread.

"You never got any messages, did you?" Martha asked.

"I did."

"Who from?" Martha asked.

Teddy's fingers picked harder. "I'd rather not say." His faced turned red.

"I bet you never got one word," Martha said. She looked at the board on her lap. She felt ridiculous. "Stop picking my spread!" she scolded, and Teddy jumped and sat on his hands.

"You're weird, Teddy Winterrab," she said in a mean voice. "Everybody says you're weird."

"So what?" Teddy cried, leaping out of the chair.

"This Ouija board is stupid," Martha shouted. "It's for little kids who believe in Santa Claus."

Teddy yelled back. "I thought you were different, Martha. I thought you would understand but you don't!"

"What on earth is going on?" Mom was at the door, peering anxiously into the room.

"She's the same as all the rest of them," Teddy said, and pushed past her. "She stinks!"

Martha's mother stood there with her mouth open. Martha avoided her eyes. "Everybody knows Teddy is weird," she said, but her voice wasn't very strong. It was the first time she'd had a real argument with a boy. Her heart was beating hard and she was very mad.

"You and your sister," Mom said. "Boys!" She went off, probably to make sure Teddy got out the door.

Martha realized the Ouija board was still on her lap. "Mysterious Oracle," it said on the edge, with pictures of ghostly figures floating through the words. The idea of getting a message from Grandpa on such a contraption seemed double ridiculous. Martha didn't know how she had ever fallen for it.

She shoved the board and the planchette back into the paper bag and pushed it way under her bed. If Teddy wanted it back, he'd have to come get it. And apologize.

Martha stared at the wall, and finally her heart calmed down.

Boring, she thought. Getting better is just as boring as being sick.

4.

Martha recuperated fast. The next day she got to stay out of bed longer, and the day after that she got dressed. It felt strange to be in clothes instead of pajamas, and the waistband of her jeans seemed miles too big.

"You poor skinny thing," her mother said. "We'll have to fatten you up again."

Jemima was always on a diet, so when she came home that afternoon, Martha told her, "I lost weight. I went down ten pounds." Jemima made a face and said, "Big deal," but she looked jealous, as if she wished she could get some strep herself.

Jemima went into the kitchen and took out the peanut butter and jelly. Martha followed her.

"That's why you're so fat," she said.

"Get lost, fart-face," Jemima said.

Martha sat down across from her at the kitchen table. "How's Mellow Rollings?" she asked.

Jemima spread five-inch layers of peanut butter on pieces of melba toast. She covered the peanut butter mounds with glops of jelly.

"Isn't he the pits!" Jemima said, laughing. "He keeps following me around." Her face got serious. "He better stop it, though. He's becoming obsessive."

"What's obsessive?" Martha asked. She liked it when Jemima forgot who she was talking to, and treated her like a human being. Martha helped herself to one of the peanut butter slabs. Jemima poured a glass of milk for each of them.

"It's when somebody keeps doing something even though they shouldn't."

Martha wondered if Teddy Winterrab qualified as obsessive. He did things he knew he shouldn't. Like the time he squirted Elmer's glue into Miss Bakeley's piano. The music teacher started to play and the keys stuck. Teddy said it was the Unfinished Symphony, but nobody, not even the other class nutcakes, thought it was funny.

"Maybe they can't help it," Martha said, remembering the look on Teddy's face when he was sent to the principal's office. It was like he couldn't believe what he'd done.

"Ha!" Jemima said, sending a spray of melba toast around the table. "They don't want to stop. Rollings has got a *biiiiig* problem if he thinks he can get anywhere with me."

Jemima dumped the dirty glasses, plates, and knives into the sink, gave the table a wipe that sent crumbs onto the floor, and went to her room and shut the door. Martha sighed, then swept up the crumbs with the broom and dustpan, feeling a little dizzy as she bent over.

The afternoon stretched out lazily. Mom was at her volunteer job. Jemima's stereo boomed from behind the bedroom door. Martha thought about homework, and about how she wished she could be obsessive about getting it done.

The doorbell rang.

30

"Who is it?" Martha asked. It was a family rule to ask *"Who is it?"* before opening the door.

"Is that you, Mrs. El?" a voice said.

Martha recognized the scratchy voice of Mrs. Morris. It was all right to let her in, but, strictly speaking, she had not answered the question of Who is it?

"Oh, it's you, Martha," Mrs. Morris said when Martha opened the door. "How are you dear? Feeling better?"

"Yes, thank you. My mother is at the hospital."

Mrs. Morris put a hand over her heart and looked alarmed. "Something's the matter?"

"No, no," Martha hastily explained. "It's her volunteer job."

Mrs. Morris fanned herself and sighed with relief. She walked right in past Martha and sat down on one of the kitchen chairs. "I'm so glad. I've had enough bad news for one day."

Martha waited, hoping Mrs. Morris would tell her the bad news. It would be more interesting than studying for the history test. But Mrs. Morris didn't say anything. She looked Martha up and down.

"Would you like a glass of water or something?" Martha asked.

"That would be nice, dear." Mrs. Morris pulled her chair in and spread her big arms across the table. "I'm having terrible trouble," she said.

"I'm sorry to hear that," Martha said as she filled a clean glass with water. She put in a couple of ice cubes, to make it look fancier.

Mrs. Morris took a gulp. Then she said, "It's the *will.* We're having such trouble over it."

Martha sat down opposite Mrs. Morris. She wasn't quite sure whose will it was, but she was prepared to listen.

"You know my husband, Mr. Morris?" Mrs. Morris asked. Martha nodded. "He had a brother named Archie, just like my son Archie. They were very fond of each other. We used to call them Big Archie and Little Archie."

Martha tried to picture tall, plump Archie Morris as Little Archie. It was hard to do. Martha liked Archie. He had gone away to college, and then had to come back when Mr. Morris had a heart attack. He worked in the family ice cream store now. He always smiled and told jokes that were funny—they weren't at all like Martha's father's jokes; and he gave the kids free tastes of the new flavors so they could decide which one to buy.

"Uncle Archie, the big one, died recently, God rest his soul," Mrs. Morris was saying. "We know he wanted to leave everything he had to Little Archie, but nobody can find the will." Mrs. Morris dabbed at her eyes with a tissue that she pulled out from the sleeve of her blouse.

It must be bad for Mrs. Morris to cry, Martha thought. She wondered if Big Uncle Archie had been rich. Probably. People only got upset about wills when a lot of money was involved. She knew that from TV. And also, when her Grandpa died, nobody worried about a will. Grandpa had hardly any money at all.

"And there's another problem," Mrs. Morris said, stuffing the tissue back up her sleeve. "Uncle Archie's ex-wife. She's claiming everything for herself."

Martha got up and refilled the glass of water. The ice

cubes were still pretty good. She put the glass back down in front of Mrs. Morris, but there was no reaction. Mrs. Morris seemed to be far away, in some gloomy funk.

Martha decided it was best to be quiet, like at a funeral. After all, Uncle Archie had died only recently.

But all of a sudden Mrs. Morris rose out of her chair, like a big whale rising out of the ocean. "It's all right," she said. "I just needed to blow off steam." She peered down at Martha. "And what am I burdening you with my troubles for! You poor sick child. Tell your mother I said hello. And when you're better, come downstairs and I'll bake you some brownies."

Mrs. Morris knew about Mom's lists of forbidden foods. She gave Martha a wink.

"I hope you find the will," Martha said as she let Mrs. Morris out the door.

Mrs. Morris stopped in her tracks and took the tissue out again.

"Fat chance!" she said. "Not with that ex-wife around." She was about to go down the stairs when she stopped and turned to Martha. "I know it sounds like we're greedy," she said quietly. "But Archie could use the money for his education. He should have a chance to finish college. He's a good boy, helping his father with the store and never thinking of himself."

"I'm really sorry," Martha said, and she meant it. She wished Archie could inherit a fortune and go back to college, even if it meant no more free samples of ice cream.

"If only we could ask Uncle Archie," Mrs. Morris said, and shook her head sadly. "But there's no telephone line to heaven." She looked up at the ceiling as if she expected to see Uncle Archie floating there.

Martha's head felt full of wool when Mrs. Morris left. I better lie down, she thought, all this socializing has worn me out.

On the way to her bedroom she went past Jemima's door, and Jemima poked her head out. "Who was that?" she asked.

"Mrs. Morris from downstairs."

"Oh." Jemima looked disappointed. "For a moment I thought it was that creep Mellow Rollings again." Jemima frowned and shut the door in Martha's face.

"I'm going to lie down in bed," Martha yelled through the closed door.

"You better not get sick again," Jemima yelled back.

"I didn't get sick on purpose," Martha shouted. "And keep your stereo down! I have to rest. You can answer the door or the phone."

Jemima turned her music up louder. Martha stomped to her bedroom. She kicked off her sneakers and got into bed, jeans and all. She pulled the covers up and closed her eyes.

Her head was spinning with Mrs. Morris's words. Poor Big Archie, poor Little Archie, poor Mellow Rollings, and poor Teddy Winterrab. People couldn't help what they did, they just did it. Like Mellow being obsessive and liking Jemima, and weird Teddy believing in a Ouija board.

Martha threw the covers off her head and sat up. She leaned over and pulled the paper bag out from under the bed.

No telephone line to heaven, Mrs. Morris had said.

An idea popped into Martha's mind. She looked at the paper bag.

"No," she told herself firmly. "It's too nutty."

5.

It was scary doing it alone. Martha wished Teddy were there, but that would be impossible. Besides, it would be losing face. She had told him she thought his Ouija board was stupid, and she couldn't take back her words now.

It felt creepy waiting to talk to a dead person. Martha was waiting under a sheet, a flashlight in one hand and the planchette in the other. So far nothing had happened.

She tried to keep her mind a blank, but all kinds of silly thoughts kept jumping in. Like the time Jenny bought two ice cream pops on the way home from school and ate both of them herself. Or the time she made Martha pick out all the biggest potato chips and then gobbled them up. Jenny was probably a vampire, just like Phyllis Blott.

She reminded herself that she should be concentrating on making contact with Uncle Archie. Even if it was a dopey thing to do, it was for Little Archie.

"Uncle Archie," she moaned softly into the dark room. "Big Archie? Are you there?"

She hoped he wouldn't turn out to be horrible. It was one thing to get a message from your own grandfather and another to contact some dead person you didn't even know.

"Uncle Archie," she whispered again. "I need a message."

Should she tell him why? Or did dead people know everything anyway?

It was annoying. Teddy hadn't given her enough details. She decided she had better explain, so she told Uncle Archie how Little Archie needed to find the will.

All of a sudden the planchette moved. Martha's hand was so sweaty, it almost slipped off the disk. She felt a tingle in her fingers and up through her arm.

Yuk, she thought, but kept her fingers on the piece of plastic. It jerked around the board so fast, she couldn't keep track of the letters.

S . . . N . . . K . . . E

Was this really happening?

The planchette moved again.

S . . . E . . . N . . . K

"Uncle Archie," she said. She hoped it *was* Uncle Archie. "You're not making any sense."

As if in reply, the planchette whipped around the board even faster.

S . . . T . . . E . . . N . . . K, it spelled.

"Rude," Martha said. "Stink yourself!"

The planchette stopped. Martha's arm quivered. Her stomach flopped.

"I'm sorry," she whispered. The flashlight battery was getting weak. It would go out and she'd be alone in the dark with a dead ghost. An angry dead ghost.

"I'm sorry I said that. It's just that it's hard for me. I'm new at this, you know!"

She put her fingers back on the plastic disk. "Please!" she whispered fiercely. The light was almost gone.

Slowly the planchette began to move again. It went from one letter to another in great slow arcs. Martha watched, squinting in the dying yellow light.

S . . . I . . N . . . K, the planchette spelled. *S . . . E . . N . . . K,* as if it couldn't make up its mind.

"Sink?" Martha asked. "Are you trying to spell *sink?*"

At the top of the board were two words enclosed in fancy circles. One said "yes" and the other said "no." Teddy had explained you could get quick answers by using these. Martha watched now, hoping the planchette would tell her yes or no about the word *sink.*

The planchette moved upward. The flashlight was dimming to almost nothing. "Hurry!" Martha almost shouted.

But as the piece of plastic reached the top of the board, the light went out.

6.

In the daylight the whole idea seemed dumb. Who would hide a will in the kitchen sink? Martha could see that communicating with the spirit world was full of problems. It was best to be sure who you were talking to before you asked questions.

It didn't matter. She'd put the board back in the paper bag and shoved it under her bed. If Teddy wanted it, he would have to come and get it, because she wasn't going to be caught taking his Ouija board to school.

Martha didn't say anything to Mrs. Morris about the sink. And Mrs. Morris seemed to have forgotten about the will anyway. She came up to talk to her mother about the problem in the laundry room instead.

"Somebody let a cat in," Mrs. Morris said. "There's a bad smell."

Martha's mom said baking soda was the best thing to get rid of bad smells.

"Whose cat was it?" Martha asked. She was in the kitchen having lunch before her mother went to her volunteer job. That morning they'd been to Martha's doctor for a checkup. He said she could go back to school the next week.

"Nobody in this building," Mrs. Morris said. "You know pets aren't allowed."

Martha knew that was the rule, but there was a canary upstairs and a guinea pig downstairs, and a large family of gerbils lived down the hall. Adults always changed the rules to suit themselves, she thought. She felt a little ornery. She looked out the window at the blue sky and white puffy clouds. "Mom? Can I go out for a while?"

Mom got flustered. "I have to leave in a minute," she said. "I don't like the idea of you being out alone when no one is home. You might have a relapse. Wait until Jemima gets home from school."

Jemima would never take her. Jemima hated to do anything after school except listen to her stereo or talk to Denise on the phone.

"The doctor said I was fine," Martha said. "And I don't need a baby-sitter."

"I tell you what," said Mrs. Morris. "I'll watch you from my window. How is that, Mrs. El? Martha will stay in sight and I'll keep my eye on her."

"That's very kind, isn't it, Marth?" Mom asked.

Martha felt sorry she hadn't been able to get a better message on the Ouija board for Mrs. Morris.

The air smelled wonderful to her after being indoors for so long. Martha felt like a person who had just been released from prison after a hundred years. She walked very gingerly, taking tiny steps. Her knees were a bit wobbly. She practiced walking like a hundred-year-old prisoner would walk.

"Let me help you," a concerned voice said. Martha felt a firm hand on her arm. It was Mrs. Bender, who looked worried. "I heard you were sick," she said, holding Martha up like a puppet.

"I'm fine," Martha said, embarrassed to be caught in her feeble-prisoner act. "I've recovered."

"Yes, I see," Mrs. Bender said uncertainly. Then she smiled. Mrs. Bender was beautiful, everybody said so. She looked too young to be the mother of Harvey Bender, a bratty kid who stepped on ants. Mrs. Bender's first name was Jessica and she looked like a movie star. Standing next to her, Martha felt like a short fat gnome.

"But you're not back in school yet?" Mrs. Bender asked. Standing a long way off was Harvey, squidging up his face the way he did when he was going to howl.

"I'm not contagious anymore," Martha said. She had a feeling Harvey had been warned to keep out of range.

"Oh, that's wonderful news," Mrs. Bender said, smiling her movie-star smile. "That means Jemima can babysit again. Will you tell her I need her tomorrow night?"

"Sure," Martha said.

Harvey let out the beginning of a wail, but Mrs. Bender got there in time to cut him off and they went down the street. Harvey held his mother's hand and dragged his feet. He was swinging a ratty stuffed pig. Harvey never went anywhere without the snotty gray pig that Jemima said smelled of mildew.

It was hard to have a good walk when you had to keep in sight of Mrs. Morris's windows. Martha walked all around the front of her building, making a detour around the two squares of grass that were chained off so nobody would walk on them. She walked up and down the front steps twice and then had to sit down and catch her breath.

"Don't sit, you'll catch cold!" Mrs. Morris cried from her window. "Come up and I'll make you a hot chocolate."

Martha went upstairs and drank hot chocolate in the Morris kitchen. Although it was exactly the same size and shape as Martha's kitchen, it looked different. Martha's mother kept everything neat and put away. Mrs. Morris had pots and pans all over the place; some were even stored in the cold oven. On top of the refrigerator huge bags of pretzels and potato chips loomed.

Rows of glass jars on the counter were stuffed with cookies, marshmallows, nuts, and candy. Sometimes it made Martha dizzy.

Mrs. Morris added two dollops of whipped cream to Martha's cup. The hot chocolate tasted dark and rich, and Martha knew that whipped cream contained cholesterol. She drank it all up anyway and even had seconds. Mrs. Morris told her about a recipe for chicken legs in peanut butter sauce. She didn't mention Uncle Archie's will, and Martha thought it was probably best not to ask about it.

"There's your sister," Mrs. Morris said as she passed the kitchen window on her way to get some sugar cookies. "You better let her know you're here. Ask her if she wants to have some hot chocolate with us."

"Thanks," Martha said, "but I better go." She felt guilty and fat.

"There's plenty left for Jemima," Mrs. Morris said.

"She's on a diet."

"Diets!" Mrs. Morris sniffed. Before she would let Martha go, she gave her a bag of nacho chips for the journey up one flight. When Martha got to the apartment, she found Jemima lying on the couch, looking at the ceiling with a silly grin on her face.

Martha told her about baby-sitting for Mrs. Bender. Jemima let out a scream.

"I can't! Why did you tell her I could?"

"I didn't actually say you could," Martha began reasonably, but Jemima continued to scream. She jumped up from the couch and ran around the room.

"The biggest thing in my life is going to happen tomorrow night and you want me to baby-sit for Harvey Bender!" she yelled. She grabbed Martha's bag of nacho chips and stuffed one in her mouth.

"It wasn't *my* idea," Martha said, glad that Jemima had stopped screaming. "It was Mrs. Bender's idea. And what's this biggest thing anyway?"

Jemima stopped chewing and got a dreamy look on her face. It could only mean one thing. Larry Haggerty. He had asked Jemima for a date.

"Can you believe it?" Jemima threw the nacho chips on the couch and danced around. She tried dragging Martha with her, but Martha had to get the dustpan so she could get rid of the evidence. Nacho crumbs were all over the place.

"Isn't it wonderful?" Jemima said.

"Yes," Martha said. She didn't want to tell Jemima that Larry Haggerty's arms were too long. She had noticed it one day when he was walking in front of them at the mall. Jemima had spied him and got all red in the face. Larry Haggerty hadn't noticed them. Martha had seen quite clearly that his arms were way too long. Like an ape's. Well, maybe he would grow into them, she thought.

Jemima was screeching again. "So I can't possibly baby-sit tomorrow night!"

"Okay, okay," Martha said. "I'm not telling you to."

"But what am I gonna do?" Jemima wailed. "I always sit for the Benders."

"Get someone else to sit for you," Martha said. She burped. Hot chocolate didn't go with nacho chips.

"Brilliant!" Jemima said, patting Martha on the head. "You're not too dumb, kid."

Martha decided something must have happened to Jemima's brain when she turned fifteen. Even an ape could have figured out the baby-sitting problem.

Everything had been arranged by the time Mom got home. Jemima had all the answers ready about where, how, what and why she should be allowed to go on a date with Larry Haggerty, who was a senior and older than Jemima.

But Mom didn't even ask.

"You can't go," she said with finality. "Dad and I are having dinner at the Elkharts. You know that's Daddy's boss, and we can't leave Martha alone. You'll have to stay here with her."

Jemima let out such a yowl, Martha thought the apartment building would fall down.

7.

Blame it on the strep throat. Martha knew she could stay home alone, but Mom was worried she'd have a relapse or something. This business of being an invalid was a bore.

Martha went to commiserate with Jemima, but Jemima wouldn't let her in. "Get lost, fart-face," she said through the locked door. It was depressing to think of being with Jemima tomorrow night.

"I've got an idea," Martha said, shouting above the stereo. There was no answer. Martha went to the kitchen where Mom was preparing chicken legs for dinner. Maybe Mrs. Morris had given her the recipe.

"Listen, Mom," Martha said, trying to sound practical. She started to help bread the chicken. "You know that I usually can stay home alone. And I'm really not sick anymore." She could see her mother was about to protest, so she hurried on. "It's not fair for Jemima to have to baby-sit for me. And anyway I'm too big. Why don't we check with Mrs. Morris and see if she can keep an eye on me tomorrow night? Then Jemima can go on her date."

"Well," Mom said. "It depends if Mrs. Morris wouldn't mind."

"She didn't mind today. She can call me up every hour on the hour or something like that."

"I'd feel better if you went downstairs and stayed in her apartment," Mom said. "We wouldn't be too late."

Martha thought of drinking more cups of hot chocolate with whipped cream. "I think I could stay up here," she said.

Mom rinsed her hands off and dried them on a towel. "I know I'm sounding overprotective," she said slowly. "But the truth is, the cat got into the laundry room because someone broke in. I'm a little concerned."

"I can lock the door and not open it for anyone," Martha said. Probably some kids were just horsing around downstairs, like when they broke the sign that said GRAPE HILL APARTMENTS. "Anyway," she added hastily so Mom wouldn't have second thoughts, "can I tell Jemima it's all right?"

"Yes, I think so," Mom said, and went back to breading the chicken. "Marth?" she called, as Martha went out of the kitchen. "That was nice of you, you know. You're a good sister."

You don't know the half of it, Martha thought. She was beginning to feel like Jemima's mother. She knocked at her door, and before Jemima could yell "Go away," she shouted, "I've got good news!"

"Sure," Jemima said, opening the door only a crack and peering out with a red eye. "Tell us about it, kiddo."

"You can go out with Larry Haggerty Saturday night."

The door swung open and Jemima's face went into contortions. "You mean it?" she screeched.

"Would I lie? I arranged for Mrs. Morris to baby-sit for me." Martha expected at least a little gratitude, but all

Jemima did was go back into her room and jump around on the carpet. Then she barged past, almost knocking Martha off her feet. "I gotta call Denise!" she said.

Now I know how martyrs feel, Martha thought. She liked Mrs. Morris and her snacks and all, but she'd never live it down if Jenny knew she needed a baby-sitter. But what difference did it make? Jenny wouldn't find out because Martha wasn't ever going to talk to her again. Come to think of it, it was another advantage of not having friends. Nobody could find out the embarrassing stuff about you.

On Saturday Jemima started getting ready for her date at eight A.M. She went to the health club early so she could work off all the flab that had grown in the past week. When she came back, she took a shower and washed her hair. She spent the rest of the morning trying on clothes.

Martha stayed in bed until her mother asked if she was ever going to get up again. They had tuna sandwiches for lunch. Then Mom took a shower, washed her hair, put it up on rollers and borrowed Jemima's hair dryer. Then Dad took a shower. Martha figured he washed his hair, too, except that he didn't make a fuss about it.

Jemima put purple and silver eye makeup on and looked in the mirror and screamed, "No way, Jose!" She ran back into the shower.

Everybody was bustling around getting ready. Everybody except Martha. She only had Mrs. Morris to look forward to. At least there was the possibility of gobbling Nachos and drinking Coke.

Martha was lying down again for a nap when her father came in.

"How's my girl?" he asked.

"I'm fine," Martha said.

He sat down on the bed. "You don't sound fine," he said.

"I'm going back to school on Monday."

He laughed. "Worried about catching up on your work? You'll see, you'll be glad to be back in the swing of things."

Dad didn't really understand. She wanted to tell him how awful it was going to be, to go back and face Jenny and Phyllis Blott. But Dad always said things like "Keep a stiff upper lip" and "Don't let the turkeys get you down." Martha didn't think she wanted to hear about the turkeys right now.

"I guess I'll catch up on the work," she said instead.

"Sure you will!" he said, and patted her arm. "That's my smart girl!"

Well, at least she was a lot smarter than Jemima who was now moaning about dropping her spot stick in the toilet. Jemima used spot stick to cover up her zits. She had only a few minuscule ones on her forehead and chin, but she acted like she was a walking pox.

"Fish it out and wash it off," Mom said.

"Yuk!" Jemima said. "I'm not putting my hand in there."

"Well, you better get it out, or we'll have trouble with the plumbing."

"I better go and see if I can help," Dad said. Martha thought he looked a little tired. She wondered if he was looking forward to going to his boss's house for dinner.

By six-thirty everybody was ready. Jemima and Mom and Dad were wearing their best clothes and trying not to sit down or get them wrinkled. Jemima and Mom had their special faces on, and they almost looked like movie stars, like Mrs. Bender.

Finally the buzzer rang from downstairs. Larry Haggerty had arrived.

"Can I just go down and meet him, Mom, *please?*" Jemima begged.

"It's nicer if he comes up to meet us," Dad said.

"It makes a better impression," Mom added.

Martha didn't want to witness the horrible scene of Larry Haggerty shaking hands, with his overlong arms. She slipped out of the living room and went to her bedroom. She heard Dad's voice boom: "Good to meet you, Larry!" There was a mumble and Jemima gave a screechy laugh.

After they'd gone, Martha was delivered to the Morris apartment, feeling like a package. Mrs. Morris opened the door wearing an apron and holding a wooden spoon.

"Just in time!" she exclaimed. "Dinner is on the table."

"Bye," Martha said. Her parents went down the steps to the glass doors of the lobby. Dad held the door open and Mom turned and waved, then Martha felt herself being tugged away.

"It's a celebration!" Mrs. Morris said as she ushered Martha to the table. They were eating in the dining el instead of the kitchen, so it must be something big. The table was set with a white cloth and sparkling china and glass, and there was a vase of flowers in the center.

"Hi there, Martha," said Mr. Morris. He held a big carving knife in one hand and a big carving fork in the other.

"Hi ya," said Archie who looked different without his ice cream shop apron and cap.

"Hi," Martha said, taking her seat. She was sorry she hadn't been warned. She would have dressed up if she had known. She could have been part of the afternoon bustle.

"Sit down, sit down, everyone," Mrs. Morris said as she came out of the kitchen carrying a big platter. Everyone was already sitting.

Archie poured wine into the Morris glasses and soda into Martha's. The Morrises raised their glasses for a toast, and Martha lifted hers too.

"To Uncle Archie!" they said, and clinked glasses. Everybody took a sip.

"Isn't it wonderful, Martha?" Mrs. Morris said. "Uncle Archie's will was found! Now Archie can go back to college!"

"And we can get a manager for the store," said Mr. Morris.

"Have some mashed potatoes," Mrs. Morris said to Martha.

Martha scooped out some of the fluffy potatoes. A question was burning in her mind, but she wondered if it was polite to ask it.

But Mrs. Morris was already answering the question for her.

"They found the will in the dining room. It was right in front of their noses."

Oh, Martha thought, taking a slice of meat from the platter Mr. Morris was offering. She was glad she hadn't made a fool of herself by giving them the sink clue from the Ouija board.

"It was in the old dry sink," Mr. Morris confided, passing the platter to Archie. "And not exactly under their noses. In a secret drawer. We might never have discovered it."

Martha's fork clattered to her plate. Her hand was shaking and she stuck it down in her lap so nobody would notice.

"Everything all right, dear?" Mrs. Morris asked.

"Terrific," said Martha. Everything was fine, except that she wanted to call Teddy Winterrab on the phone right that very minute.

8.

The possibilities were mind-boggling, Martha thought as she sat on the couch between Mr. Morris and Archie, watching television. If it was so easy to summon someone from the spirit world, you could find out almost anything. Just suppose you could ask a spirit to go into Mrs. Gold's classroom and look up the answers to the history test and then come back and tell you?

Of course, it would take an awful long time to spell it all out on the Ouija board. The trouble was, there was nobody to discuss this with. It wasn't the kind of thing you could ask just anybody. They'd think you were weird. Like Teddy Winterrab. He was the only one she could ask.

Martha was prepared for another couple of hours of sitting on the Morris couch. She didn't mind watching TV, although it wasn't the program she'd watch at home; but she didn't think she could stand any more food. Mrs. Morris kept coming in with new things. Martha had already consumed an apple, two oatmeal cookies, a chocolate after-dinner mint, and three grapes. On the coffee table in front of her was a half-finished glass of soda. She had finished the first glass, and Mrs. Morris had immediately filled it up again.

The buzzer sounded, and Mrs. Morris went to the intercom. "It's Jemima!" she said.

Martha was amazed.

She looked at the Morris cuckoo clock. It was only a quarter to nine. Nobody had expected Jemima to be home from the biggest thing in her life until eleven.

"Did you have a good time, dear?" Mrs. Morris asked.

"Sure. Where's Martha?" Jemima said abruptly. Her face looked strange. She was all hot and sweaty, too, like she'd been running.

"Here I am," Martha said quickly, and jumped up from the couch.

"Stay a few minutes," Mrs. Morris said to Jemima. "I'll put some tea water on."

"No, thanks," Jemima said, and bit her lip as if she were about to cry.

"We better go," Martha said. "I have a lot of homework to catch up on. I'll never get it done by Monday morning."

"Well, all right," said Mrs. Morris. She gave them a plastic bag filled with cookies and grapes, as if they were going on an expedition instead of just one flight upstairs. "Make sure you lock your doors," Mrs. Morris warned.

Back in their apartment Martha asked cautiously, "What happened?" She wasn't sure Jemima would bother to answer, but she was dying to know. It had to be something rotten about Larry Haggerty.

"You wouldn't believe it!" Jemima cried.

"We were going to the movies, right? Well, we were early, so after we got the tickets, he says, 'Let's play a couple of video games before the show.' So we go in the game room, and a whole bunch of his friends were there." Jemima took time out to wipe her nose. Acting like Mrs. Morris, Martha put the kettle on and got the tea mugs out.

"Right away he starts goofing around with those guys. It was like I wasn't even there. They have this running contest on who can rack up the most points for Cosmic Dragons, and he got really into it. Finally I reminded him the movie was starting, and you know what he said?" Jemima's voice rose to a squeak. Martha waited. "He said he was on a roll and I should go in without him!"

Jemima's face was turning dangerously red, so Martha hurriedly poured lukewarm water on the tea bags and stuck a mug under Jemima's nose.

"So I said I thought we had a date for the movies and didn't he care about that, and he said if I cared about him I'd want to watch him zap the Galactic Motrons, and I said, 'are you coming with me or not?' and he said he'd think about it, and all his friends laughed. So I left."

Jemima blew her nose like a hoot owl into a tissue. "I walked home! I kept thinking he would run after me, but . . ." She threw the crumpled tissue at the wastebasket across the room and made a bull's-eye. "The heck with Larry Haggerty," she said.

Martha was thinking. "Maybe he's the same as Mellow Rollings. You know, obsessive, like you said. Mellow is obsessive about you, and Larry is obsessive about Cosmic Dragons."

"I don't want to talk about it anymore," Jemima said. "And listen, don't say anything to Mom and Dad, okay? It's too embarrassing."

"I won't tell," Martha promised, and crossed little fingers with Jemima. They hadn't done that in a long time.

It was sort of nice having Jemima be dependent. She didn't act so snotty.

Martha looked at the clock. It was almost ten, pretty late. Maybe she could take a chance.

"Jemima? Could I ask you a favor?"

"Sure. What?" Jemima said from inside the freezer. She was rummaging for a box of miniature frozen pizzas. Larry Haggerty was supposed to take her for pizza after the movie.

"Could you phone Teddy Winterrab's house for me? It's sort of late and I don't want to get him into trouble. But maybe if you talked to his mother, you could say that I had to ask him something about the homework, and if it wasn't too late and he was still up, could I speak to him?"

Jemima's head and the box of frozen pizzas came out of the freezer. "You don't really want to talk to him about homework, do you?"

Darn, Martha thought. She could feel her face blushing. "No," she admitted, and left it at that.

Jemima started crowing in her usual way, jumping around the kitchen like a nut.

"I don't believe it, my little baby sister has a boyfriend!"

"Oh, shut up," Martha said, but quietly because she wanted the favor.

Jemima didn't tease her too much. She couldn't because Martha knew about Larry Haggerty. So she looked up the phone number in the directory and called.

Unfortunately, she put on her phony grown-up voice and asked, "Is this the Winterrab residence?"

Somebody talked on the other end, and Jemima raised

her eyebrows. "Just a moment, then, I have a phone call for you."

She handed the phone to Martha. "Maybe he'll think it's the operator, or something. It's him." Jemima pointed at the receiver. "Your boyfriend answered the phone!" Squelching giggles, she fell onto the living room sofa.

Martha said, "Hello, Teddy? It's me, Martha. Hang on a minute." Then she did what Jemima always did. She pulled the phone into the hall bathroom and shut the door.

"Teddy? Have I got something to tell you!" she said excitedly, and it took her a moment to realize that Teddy had banged the phone down. He'd hung up right in her ear!

9.

When Monday came, Martha was ready for her new campaign. No more slipups. She'd been really dumb about Teddy, and she wouldn't make the same mistake again. It was dumb to call him, to think of him as a friend or something, when she had already made a vow not to have any friends.

Luckily she didn't have to ride the school bus the first day back. That saved having to worry about how to face Jenny. Mom thought Martha might still be too weak, and said she'd drive her. But that meant she first had to take Dad to work and bring the car back. So by the time Martha got to school, she was already late. Everybody stared at her when she came into the classroom.

Mrs. Gold made a fuss. "Look who's back! Martha Lewis!" She acted as if she hadn't seen Martha for a hundred years. Martha slunk to her seat and pretended she was busy looking for something important in her notebook. She had a feeling Jenny was staring at her, and Tessa and Diane. At least Phyllis Blott wasn't in Mrs. Gold's class.

Surprisingly, the morning went by all right, except that Martha failed the spelling test. It was lunchtime that was awful. When she walked into the lunchroom, she practically fell over Jenny and Phyllis. They were sitting at the first table, with their bags of lunch spread out.

"You can sit with us if you want," Jenny said.

Martha looked into Jenny's eyes, wondering how she could be so casual. Jenny seemed normal, like the regular old Jenny. But Martha noticed that Phyllis Blott wasn't smiling. She was stuffing a carrot stick in between her vampire teeth and looking annoyed.

"No, thanks," Martha said. "I have . . . to meet someone."

There, she'd done it. It was easy, she thought as she walked away. She hadn't even blushed or anything. She'd acted perfectly natural.

So she was surprised when her eyes started to burn a little. She sniffed hard and put down her lunch bag on an empty table in the corner. Nearby some of the sixth-grade boys were squirting milk at each other through straws. Martha sat down with her back to them. She opened up her history book and prepared to study. She had a lot of catching up to do.

"Mind if I sit here?" a voice said.

Even before she looked up, she knew who it was.

Teddy was standing there, his hair fuzzier than ever, as if he'd just rolled out of bed. He was carrying a battered Snoopy lunch box and two containers of milk in one arm and his black briefcase in the other.

"It's a free country," Martha said.

Teddy sat down. He snapped open his lunch box and took out three foil-wrapped sandwiches, a plastic container of macaroni salad, and an apple. He unwrapped the sandwiches slowly, smacking his lips. He noticed Martha staring.

"Peanut butter and banana. Want one?"

Martha shook her head.

Martha would have changed tables, but she didn't want to draw attention to herself. If she stayed where she was, maybe Jenny and Phyllis wouldn't notice. She'd told them she was meeting someone and they'd think it was *him!*

She crouched down as low as she could without sliding under the table.

"Listen," Teddy said conversationally, his mouth full of sandwich. "I'm sorry about Saturday night."

"Don't mention it," Martha said. She could hardly believe Windbag was apologizing.

"It's just that I was making this recipe. For chocolate devil's food cake. And I forgot to put the eggs in. I found them just as you called, behind the cookbook. So I took the cake out of the oven and beat the eggs around in the dough and stuck it back." Teddy finished one sandwich and started on another. "It didn't work out too well."

"Better luck next time," Martha said.

"I'm baking brownies next. The cake sort of tasted like brownies anyway. Very flat brownies."

"Do you cook a lot?" Martha asked, curiosity getting the better of her.

"Oh, sure," Teddy said. "I have to. My mother goes away a lot of weekends."

"She leaves you alone?"

"Oh, sure," Teddy said again. "I'm old enough."

Martha wondered about Teddy's father, but she didn't think it was polite to ask about him. It occurred to her that maybe Teddy's father had died and that's why he got the Ouija board, to try to get a message from his dad.

Martha felt bad that she had been mean. But, on the other hand, Teddy could have at least called her back.

"You're probably wondering why I didn't call you back," Teddy said.

Martha dropped her granola bar.

"The reason is," he went on, "I wasn't sure if your parents would get mad, since it was late. See, I've had a lot of problems with parents. They don't like me. And your mother had already given me the geeze."

"The geeze?"

"Yeah, you know, a big disapproving look. When we had that argument in your room. By the way, you wouldn't say that I was entirely at fault, would you? I think we had that argument together, fifty-fifty, right?"

Martha nodded. Teddy seemed pleased. He smiled his crooked-tooth smile.

"So when I saw you were sitting here by yourself instead of with the Nose," he said, "I decided it was my chance to apologize for hanging up."

The Nose? Martha couldn't help it, she turned around to stare at Jenny. How come she had never noticed Jenny's nose before? She stifled a giggle.

"You have an argument with her too?" Teddy was asking.

Martha quickly turned back. Jenny hadn't noticed, she was busy talking to Phyllis. They had their heads close together.

"Sort of," Martha said, thinking about how she could get out of the lunchroom quick.

Teddy nodded as if he understood everything. "I've had arguments with about ninety-nine percent of the school."

"Why?" Martha blurted out.

Teddy shrugged. "It just seems to be a habit with me," he said. "With you, too, I guess, huh?"

Martha was annoyed. "No, as a matter of fact it isn't." She stuck her half-eaten granola bar back into her lunch bag and scrunched it up into a ball. "I gotta go."

"Oh," Teddy said. He looked disappointed but tried to hide it by taking a big swig of milk. "But what about what you wanted to tell me?"

"Huh?"

" 'Have I got something to tell you,' you said. I've been wondering about it ever since. I called you back on Sunday but nobody answered."

Every Sunday they went to Grandma's house. Martha had almost wanted to tell Grandma about the Ouija board, to say that maybe they could get a message from Grandpa. But she didn't. Still, the feeling of excitement in her stomach had been there, like a goblin. She had been sorry she had nobody to share the feeling with.

Now, as Martha looked into Teddy's expectant, peanut-butter-smeared face, the excitement came rushing back. Teddy was the only one she could tell.

Still. It was Teddy Windbag. And Jenny and Phyllis would see. "It was nothing," Martha said. "I mean, I wanted to apologize, too, that's all." She felt ashamed but relieved.

Teddy's eyes became shifty, as they did whenever an adult came into the room. He doesn't trust me anymore, Martha thought, and she was surprised that it bothered her.

"Fine," he said. He picked up his third sandwich and bit into it. He acted as if she wasn't there.

"See you," Martha said in a small voice. She got up from the table and took her crumpled bag and empty milk carton to the trash barrel. At that moment Jenny and Phyllis came up behind her and flung their bags in behind Martha's.

Jenny gave Martha a scathing look. "Honestly, Marth, sitting at the same table with that creep."

"Really," Phyllis Blott said, showing her vampire fangs.

"I mean, you can always feel welcome with us," Jenny said. "If you have no one to sit with. We wouldn't mind, would we, Phyll?"

"Really," Phyllis Blott said, but she looked as if she would.

"I mean, we just don't think you should associate with people like that," Jenny said. "Otherwise people might start to think you're a creep too."

Phyllis Blott gave a croaky laugh and hid her big teeth behind her hand.

Martha felt like throwing them both into the trash barrel. Instead she heard herself saying, "What's it to you? It just so happens, Teddy Winterrab is my friend!"

10.

She couldn't believe what she'd done. Telling everybody she was a friend of Teddy's, and he didn't even know it.

"Gosh, are you really friends with Windbag?" Tessa asked when they were forming into math groups after lunch.

"Well . . ." Martha said. It would be easy to say it was all a mistake.

"You have to admit, he is weird," Diane said.

"You wouldn't want to become weird too," Tessa said.

"It's not contagious like a strep throat," Martha said.

Diane and Tessa took a step back. They had looks on their faces. Martha knew they'd avoid her if she stuck to her guns about Teddy. She didn't even want to!

"It was all a mistake!" she blurted out.

Tessa and Diane exchanged glances of relief. "We knew you weren't that dumb," they said.

"Who's dumb?" Jenny asked, coming up behind them.

"Nobody. It was a mistake about Martha and Teddy Winterrab," Tessa said.

Jenny smiled down her long nose. "Good," she said.

Tessa, Diane, and Jenny beamed at her. They looked pleased. Martha felt rotten.

She was glad she didn't have to ride the school bus home. Mom was picking her up. Martha wondered if she should try to talk to her mother about friends. But when she got into the car, she noticed the very serious look on Mom's face.

She wondered if it was worry-serious or angry-serious. She thought about all the forbidden snacks she'd been eating at Mrs. Morris's.

"Something wrong?" she asked.

"What? Oh, sorry, Marth. Yes, I might as well tell you. It's the laundry room again. The super fixed the lock and now the window has been jimmied."

Martha relaxed. "Is that all?"

"Martha! It means someone is breaking in!"

"But there's nothing to steal in the laundry room," Martha said.

"Don't be obtuse. Once they get in there, they can get into the whole building."

"Has anyone been robbed?" Martha asked, feeling a little scared for the first time.

"Not yet. But something's going on. Maybe a tramp is sleeping in there at night."

That gave Martha the creeps. After dinner she and Jemima often went down to get the wash out of the dryer. Martha didn't like the idea of stepping on a tramp.

"I didn't mean to alarm you," Mom said. "It could just be kids. But it's wise to take precautions."

"Like what?"

"Keep all the doors locked. Don't answer if you don't know who it is. Be sure to use the intercom before you buzz anybody in."

"We do all that already," Martha said, but Mom wasn't paying attention.

"If only we could find out who it was," she was saying, "I'd feel better. I hate not knowing whether it's just a prank or a real burglar."

"Maybe the police could stake the place out," Martha suggested. That's what they did on TV.

"They can't be bothered with our laundry room. They said we should organize the tenants to watch. But nobody wants to spend the night down there." Mom looked annoyed. "The truth is, neither do I."

"You need closed-circuit TV," Martha said.

"Or eyes in the backs of our heads. Or ESP. Honestly, Martha, if you can't say something practical, don't say anything at all. I'm not in the mood for jokes."

"Okay, okay," Martha said, and slumped down in the seat. "But it wasn't a joke."

Mom glared. Martha closed her mouth.

A police stakeout and closed-circuit TV were a lot more sensible than ESP. Who the heck had ESP at 1804 Grape Hill Apartments?

"Me!" Martha said.

"What now?" Mom said.

"Nothing."

The Ouija board, of course. The spirits wouldn't mind hanging out in the laundry room, would they? She could ask them to help. A spirit stakeout. But was it the kind of thing you could ask spirits to do?

She didn't have enough information to work with. She needed Teddy. It looked like she would have to be friends with him whether she liked it or not.

She decided to call him as soon as she got home. But

Jemima got there first, and hogged the phone all afternoon, talking to Denise about what a jerk Larry Haggerty was. Martha could tell that Jemima didn't really mean it. She loved Larry Haggerty in spite of their rotten date.

Finally Martha pulled the phone into the bathroom and called. Teddy answered. Before he could hang up, Martha blabbed out an apology. Apologies were getting to be a habit with them.

"I'm sorry I didn't tell you in school," she said. "But I was afraid to talk in public."

"About what?" Teddy sounded distant and cold.

"The Ouija board."

"What about it?"

Martha told him about Uncle Archie's will.

Teddy listened quietly until she was done. "You have to watch out for coincidence," he said. "Just because the missing will turned up in a dry sink doesn't mean you received a message from Uncle Archie himself."

"That would be some coincidence," Martha said. "How are we supposed to know when it is or isn't?"

"You have to keep a scientific notebook," Teddy explained, "so that you can check on yourself. You see, the mind plays tricks. You hear about the Morris will being found and you really believe you got the word *sink* from the board. But it could be you're only imagining that you did."

"Let me get this straight," Martha said. "You mean that I didn't get the word *sink* at all? That after I heard about the will being found, I talked myself into believing I'd received *sink* as a message?"

"That's it," Teddy said.

"But that isn't it! I know what I got. I knew it for two

days before I ever heard about the will. I didn't dream it up." Martha's voice was rising. She felt upset. She didn't like the idea that her imagination could be playing tricks.

"Don't get mad," Teddy said. "All I mean is that it could happen. But if you keep a notebook and write everything down with a date, then nobody can call you a liar."

Martha calmed down a little.

"Still," she said, "I did get some message, even if it wasn't the right one. The planchette did move, Teddy!"

"I wish you'd call it a pusher," he said. "And I hate to tell you, but you could have moved it yourself."

"What? First you tell me that stupid old board is guaranteed to get messages from the dead, and now you tell me I'm sending messages to myself. Listen here, Teddy Winterrab, are you pulling one of your weird stunts with me?!"

There was silence at the other end, but she knew he hadn't hung up.

"Teddy? You still there?"

"I'm not talking to you if you're mad."

"I'm not mad."

"Yes you are."

"I'm not mad!" Martha screamed into the phone. She heard footsteps outside the bathroom door. "I'm fine, I'm calm," she whispered.

"I just wanted to make sure you knew the pitfalls," Teddy said.

"Okay, I understand. I guess you have to be scientific in a case like this."

"Now you're cooking," Teddy said.

"I'll get a notebook. But I need to know a few things

now. I have a lot of questions I want to get answered, and I'm not sure who to contact. You said I should talk to people I know. But I don't know who knows the answers."

There was a pause. Teddy seemed to be thinking. "You're not scared of ghosts, are you?"

"Why?"

"Well, I should also tell you that you don't always get in touch with the person you ask for. Sometimes other spirits just barge in and give messages. Some of them can be a little unfriendly."

"What do you mean unfriendly?" Martha had a funny feeling in her stomach.

"Are you scared?"

"Of course I'm not scared," she said, giving the bath-tub a kick. "These spirits don't show up in person, do they?"

"Well, no, I don't think so," Teddy said.

"You don't sound too sure."

"I've never seen any. But some people are called medi-ums. That means they have the ability to reach spirits better than anyone else. You could be a medium, Martha, if you really got that message about the sink so quick."

"I told you I did," Martha said, and then stopped. A medium? Her? Her stomach churned.

"Do you think it could be true?" she asked.

"Anything's possible," Teddy said.

"Gosh," Martha said. Think of the possibilities. Think of the answers she could get!

"Listen, I gotta go," Teddy was saying, "my mother wants to use the phone. We can talk about it some more in school tomorrow."

71

"Okay, sure," Martha said, still thinking about getting answers to the history test and solving the mystery of the laundry room. It was only after she heard the buzz in her ear that she remembered Teddy's last few words. Talk about it some more in school tomorrow!

Martha groaned. How was she going to make him understand there was no way she could be seen talking to him in school!

11.

Martha woke up with a sick feeling that had nothing to do with strep throat. Two horrible prospects loomed: Windbag and the Nose. She would have to ignore the Nose on the school bus and ignore Teddy in school.

How had she become friends with Jenny anyway? Their parents moved to Grape Hill when the apartments were brand-new. Lots of people came out to Grape Hill to get away from the dirt and smog of the city. It was an easy commute, you could walk to the mall, and there were plenty of parks. Until the apartments were built, Grape Hill had been only private homes and woods.

Their mothers used to take them to the park, and Jenny and Martha played together. They went to each other's birthday parties. They started school together. Maybe the only reason they became friends was because their mothers wanted them to be.

Jenny always said she'd rather live in one of the private houses instead of an apartment. She always wanted to own a dog and a cat. She liked watching horror movies on TV, and once they both saw fifty cents lying on the sidewalk and Jenny ran and grabbed it and wouldn't share it with Martha.

Martha didn't mind living in an apartment, and cats

and dogs were nice, but she didn't pine for them. She liked movies about space and scientists making great discoveries, and she would have given Jenny half of the fifty cents if she had picked it up first. Maybe all this time she had been friends with someone she didn't even like!

Jenny was already at the bus stop when Martha got there.

"Hi," she said.

"Hello, Jenny," Martha said, making her voice sound like her father's when he talked business on the phone. "How are you today?"

Jenny looked startled. "Ummm, fine thanks," she said.

The bus came, and Martha took a seat far away from Jenny. She opened her math book and pretended to study.

When they got to school, there was Teddy waiting at the entrance, watching all the kids getting off the buses. Martha squatted down in the middle of a bunch of second-graders and waddled off with them. Then she ran like heck around the corner to the gym door.

At lunch he was waiting at an empty table. She saw him before he saw her, so she quickly looked the other way. Out of the corner of her eye she noticed his hand waving and pointing. She sidled along the edge of the lunchroom, pretending to be busy looking for something on the floor.

"Hey, Martha!" he called. Everybody heard.

She ran to the girls' bathroom. She locked herself in one of the cubicles and ate her lunch. It was a little disgusting, eating sprouts and tofu in the bathroom.

Teddy was lurking in front of Mrs. Gold's door after lunch period. He had a concerned, questioning look on his face. Martha could see Jenny at the other end of the hall. She was walking toward them.

"What happened to you?" Teddy asked.

"I felt sick," Martha said.

Jenny was coming nearer, eyebrows raised.

"Are you okay now?"

Jenny slipped past them, her big nose in the air.

"I gotta go," Martha said, and ran to her seat.

To avoid looking at Jenny, Martha decided to copy the homework assignments from the blackboard. When she looked up, she saw a big chalk heart with an arrow through it. "M loves T" was written inside. She heard Jenny cackle.

There wasn't even any peace when the day was over. Phyllis Blott was waiting in the bus line with Jenny, holding one of the pink slips you needed for permission to ride home with a friend.

It was against the rules, but Martha couldn't face it, so she walked home. Maybe the driver wouldn't notice, since she hadn't gone home on the bus yesterday either.

She plodded along, a little worried because it was a long walk and her knees still felt weak. She heard a voice behind her.

"Hey, wait up!"

She slowed down just a little.

He caught up with her. He walked beside her but didn't say anything. After two blocks the silence hung like a dead weight.

"Well, you're a creep, like the rest of them," Teddy said suddenly.

"What?"

"You think I don't know what's going on?" He shook his head in disgust.

"Nothing's going on," Martha mumbled.

"Sure it is. You're embarrassed to be seen with me."

It was horrible to hear him blurt out the truth. "No, I'm not," Martha said weakly.

He just gave her a sad smile.

"So what are you walking with me for if I'm so creepy?" she cried.

"Because I feel sorry for you."

"I don't need you to feel sorry for me," Martha said.

"Who else will?" Teddy asked. "The trouble with you is that you're too worried about what other people think."

"You have to be," Martha said. "I mean, you can't ignore it, can you?"

"Sure you can," Teddy said. "I've been doing it my whole life."

Martha wished he'd buzz off. She didn't want to be bothered with all this philosophy. But when he kept on walking right beside her, she had to admit it: "I'm a coward," she said. She was surprised she'd said it, but it was true.

"That's okay," Teddy said. "You have to get used to not caring what people think. It takes time. You haven't had much practice."

Martha didn't like his superior attitude. She felt confused, too. It was fine to *say* you didn't care what people thought about you. But it was another thing to really not care. Martha wasn't sure she didn't care. In fact, she wished Jenny were still her friend and that she had never gotten mixed up with Teddy Windbag. She wished it were like it was before she got strep throat.

"I get off here," Teddy said at the corner of Bailey Avenue. He pointed up the hill. "I live up there."

Martha was trapped into waiting with him while the light changed. When the Walk sign began to flash, she said "Bye," and started to hurry off.

"I'll tell you one thing," Teddy shouted. "You can be my friend when you're ready. But you gotta ask yourself if you can be yourself first."

12.

By the time Martha got home, she was in a bad mood. She'd arrived at Grape Hill at the same time as the school bus and almost bumped right into Jenny and Phyllis. No sooner had she made a detour than she bumped into Harvey Bender who smacked her with his soggy stuffed pig. Mrs. Bender came over and apologized.

"And I wonder if you could do me a favor," Mrs. Bender added. "Tell Jemima I need her Saturday afternoon. I hope she can come. Harvey didn't like the other girl at all."

Martha began to explain that she couldn't guarantee Jemima would sit, but Mrs. Bender was already pulling Harvey away.

Martha sighed. She was at the rear of number 1804 and the door to the laundry room was ajar. Without thinking much about it, Martha went in. It would save her a trip around to the front and the possibility of encountering the Nose. The Nose and the Blot.

It wasn't until she was in the dim back hall that she remembered about the lock and somebody breaking in. Here was the door, open again!

Martha shivered and looked around. She could hear clothes tumbling in one of the dryers. She peered into

the laundry room, hoping to see somebody from the building. But although the clothes were drying, nobody was there.

Remembering her mother's warnings, Martha backed out of the laundry room.

But then she saw it. A foot was sticking out from behind one of the big yellow dryers. Somebody was hiding!

She moved as quietly as she could, her eyes glued to the blue-and-gray sneaker. She prayed it wouldn't move.

She rushed into her apartment. The phone was ringing. She heard water running in the bathroom, and her mother's voice called out, "Marth, is that you? Could you answer please!"

Martha dropped her book bag and picked up the phone. A voice mumbled at the other end.

"Who?" Martha asked. "I'm sorry, I can't hear you."

"Jemima," the voice said, barely audible.

If Jemima had been home, the phone would have been answered in a split second. "Sorry," Martha said. "She's not here. Can I take a message?" But almost before she finished speaking, the line went dead.

Mom came out of the bathroom, rubbing her hair dry with a big pink towel.

"Who was that?" Mom asked.

"Somebody for Jemima," Martha said. "You just missed him," she told Jemima, who was just coming in the door.

"Him!" her sister cried. "Who?"

"He didn't say."

"Him!" Jemima looked ecstatic. Probably thinking it was Larry Haggerty. Then she frowned. Probably realizing it could have been somebody else.

"There's a casserole in the oven for you two," Mom said. "We're having a tenants' meeting at the Morrises, to discuss the problem of the laundry room."

Martha wondered if she should tell her mother that the door was open again and that she had seen a blue-and-gray sneaker hiding behind the dryer. It would mean getting a lecture about coming in the back door and not taking precautions.

"We're going to organize a patrol," Mom said. "The men will take turns, until we find out who it is. In the meantime I want you two girls to be careful."

"Oh, Moooom," Jemima said, tossing her head. "We're not babies."

"This could be serious, Jemima," Mom said. "Better safe than sorry."

"There already is a patrol," Martha said. Grape Hill Apartments had its own security force: men in gray uniforms who walked on the grass when nobody else was allowed to.

Mom frowned. "So far they haven't done much," she said. "The tenants have finally agreed to take action themselves."

Jemima gave a shrug, then went to her room and closed the door. In a minute the *boom-boom* of her stereo seeped out.

"I hope *you'll* be sensible, Martha," Mom said, and Martha was glad she hadn't confessed. She had agreed with Jemima that it was a lot of fuss over nothing but there was something really creepy about someone hiding in the laundry room. Anybody who was innocent wouldn't hide like that. She was glad they were organizing a patrol.

She and Jemima ate the casserole in the living room so they could watch television. TV wasn't allowed at meals, except when they could get away with it.

They were engrossed in a *Star Trek* rerun that Martha had already seen fifteen times when the sounds of a commotion interrupted Captain Kirk's discussion with Mr. Sulu.

"What's going on?" Jemima said.

Martha heard the sharp crackle of a car radio, and when she went to the window, she saw a police car parked outside, its red light flashing.

"They must have caught him!" she said. "Come on!"

They left their plates on the living room couch and the TV blasting, and ran down to the basement.

There was Archie Morris hanging on to one arm of a teenaged boy and a policeman hanging on to the other. The boy didn't look as if he wanted to struggle. But he was red in the face, and his mouth was open in protest. Jemima's mouth dropped open when she saw him.

"Mellow Rollings," she said.

"Hi, Jemima," he replied in a miserable voice. "Could you tell them I'm not doing anything."

"You've been trespassing, young man," one of the tenants scolded.

"You've been breaking the lock to get in here!" somebody else added.

"I didn't!" Mellow protested, and he looked at Jemima with big, pleading eyes. Jemima backed off, as if she didn't want to be responsible.

Martha's dad pushed through the crowd. "Maybe you can tell us what you were doing here, then," he said. "You don't live in this building, do you?"

Mellow shook his head sadly. He grew even redder in the face and stared at the floor.

"Well?" Martha's dad asked. The other tenants were growing impatient. One or two grumbled that the police should take Mellow away and lock him up.

Finally Mellow mumbled in a voice so low only those closest could hear, "I came to see her."

"What's that?" somebody asked.

"Who?" asked Martha's dad.

"Her," Mellow said, and raised his chin. He pointed at Jemima with the arm that Archie held. Jemima turned bright red and ran away.

Mom spoke up. "That could be true. Mellow was here once before waiting to see my daughter."

Mrs. Morris nodded in agreement.

"Breaking locks is a crime, no matter what the reason," a tenant said, and roused the crowd into angry grumblings again.

"But I didn't break any locks," Mellow said. "The door was open."

While this was going on, Martha had been looking at Mellow's feet. Mellow wore sneakers . . . *white* sneakers. Mellow hadn't been hiding behind the dryer this afternoon.

"He didn't do it," she said, but nobody heard her. She cleared her throat, then raised her voice and said it again.

Everybody stopped talking and stared at her.

Mom got ready to say something, so Martha went on in a hurry.

"I was in here this afternoon and somebody was hiding." She explained about the shoes.

The policeman looked down at Mellow's white sneakers. Then he asked gruffly, "Tell me, kid, do you own a pair of blue-and-gray sneakers?"

"Uh, uh, uh, no," Mellow said, sounding less than sure. The policeman's grip tightened again.

"Wait!" Martha said, not believing she was actually arguing with the police. The policeman glared at her.

"What were you doing at three-thirty this afternoon?" she asked Mellow in a shaky voice.

Mellow shuffled his feet. He made more *uh* sounds. At last he answered, "I phoned Jemima."

"That's the truth!" Martha said triumphantly. "I know because I answered the phone. And if Mellow was home making a phone call, he couldn't have been here in the laundry room."

A few of the tenants smiled. Martha felt pleased with herself. And then some big mouth said, "That doesn't prove a thing. There's a pay phone right outside the building."

Mellow was dragged off by the police. "I didn't do it!" he kept saying as he was put into the police car.

Martha felt sorry for him. It must be terrible to be accused of a crime you didn't commit. She wished there was some way she could really prove that Mellow was innocent. But the only way she could do that would be to find out who owned a pair of blue-and-gray sneakers.

The answer popped into her mind probably because it was there all along anyway. The Ouija board. She hadn't had time to get the scientific notebook, and to tell the truth, she had been feeling a little nervous about being a medium. But she'd have to do it. It was for an important cause.

13.

When everyone went to bed and it was dark and quiet, she got her equipment together: flashlight, new batteries, Ouija board, planchette, pencil, and paper.

She'd start with Uncle Archie, since he'd helped before.

"Uncle Archie?" she called softly. "Are you there? It's me, Martha."

The planchette stayed right where it was on the board, glued to her sweaty left finger. Her right hand held the pencil over the pad, ready to take down the letters.

"Uncle Archie, I have to ask you an important question. It's a matter of life and death, if you'll excuse the expression."

Nothing.

Her faith was dwindling again.

The planchette slid ever so slightly across the board. "Hello?"

It slid back. Martha felt a shiver. Had the room become colder? She waited, almost holding her breath, but the planchette was still for so long, Martha thought it had been her own nervous energy that had moved it. But then it started to swing all over the board, hitting letters so fast, Martha couldn't take them down.

"Hold your horses!" she finally cried in exasperation.
The planchette stopped dead.

"I'm sorry I yelled, Uncle Archie," she said. "But I only have two hands."

Furiously the planchette whizzed to the word *NO* and stayed there, bouncing up and down.

"No what? No, you don't believe I'm sorry?"

Bam bam bam, went the piece of plastic.

"Okay, okay. But whatever's bugging you, you'll have to tell me more slowly."

The planchette began to spell, slowly, the word *HELLO.*

"Hello, Uncle Archie," Martha said. In an instant her finger was whisked back to *NO.* Again the plastic piece jumped up and down.

This time Martha figured it out. "You're not Uncle Archie, are you?" She felt a slight sinking sensation, and she was sure the room was very cold now.

"Who are you, then?" She would try to keep an unscared mind.

The planchette sped to the top of the board where it said "Mystifying Oracle" under the picture of the moon and stars.

"That's who you are?" Martha asked.

The planchette sped away to spell out *HA HA.*

Martha got mad. She hadn't realized spirits could act as silly as people. "Be serious," she said.

WHY? the planchette spelled.

"Because I haven't got much time," Martha said impatiently. "You see this flashlight? It runs on batteries. And when the batteries run down, the light goes out and I can't see a thing!"

SILLY, the planchette spelled. *I CAN SEE IN THE DARK.*

"Good for you," Martha grumbled. "Whoever you are."

The planchette sailed across the alphabet in a dainty way. *PINKY,* it spelled.

"Is that your name? Okay, Pinky, I'm pleased to meet you. My name is Martha. I have something important to ask you."

Ignoring Martha's words, the planchette moved across the board, spelling rapidly: *PLEASED TO MEET YOU TOO.*

"Okay, that's nice, but can we get down to business? What I need to know is, who was hiding in the laundry room this afternoon?"

HOW SHOULD I KNOW? Pinky spelled.

Martha's teeth were chattering now, the room was so cold. "This is serious!" she cried in consternation. The planchette slipped off the board and onto the bed, as if it were pouting.

"I'm sorry," Martha said in her best polite voice. "I know you must be busy. I won't keep you much longer. I just wondered if you happened to know who was in the laundry room. You see, it's important. They arrested the wrong person." Hopefully now, Martha put the planchette back on the board.

A PUZZLE, Pinky promptly spelled.

"Yes, it is," Martha agreed.

The planchette didn't move. Martha shivered.

"Are you still there? Pinky?"

I'M THINKING, Pinky spelled.

Martha waited. She could hardly stand it.

"I'm freezing," she said.

The planchette tapped and she knew Pinky was mad.

MY FINAL WORD, Pinky said, and spelled: *TRY ARCHEES WANGLE GAME.*

"What?" Martha asked. "What's this? This isn't about Archie, that was last time. This is about the laundry room. Pinky?"

The planchette was lifeless. The room was growing warmer.

"Pinky! You rat!" Martha cried. "Come back here and explain."

There was a whoosh, as if a fast-moving train had roared past Martha's head. She felt her hair blow up and her scalp tingle. *Whoosh.* The train went around the room, knocking over knickknacks and spilling a mugful of pencils across the floor. The curtains swirled and the windowpanes banged. Then everything went quiet.

Martha kept her eyes shut tight until she was sure it had gone. Ghosts could sure get mad. She would remember to stay on their good side from now on.

14.

Martha had no appetite the next morning. She'd felt all right when she first opened her eyes, and then she saw the knocked-over knickknacks and the pencils on the floor, and her teeth chattered.

I have actually talked to a ghost, she thought, and her bones began to rattle.

"You feeling okay?" Dad asked.

"No fever again, I hope!" Mom said, patting her head.

"She's in love," Jemima said with a smirk, but Martha gave her a warning look and she clammed up.

"I'm fine," Martha told her parents. They didn't believe her, she could see it in their eyes. "I'm scared. I have a big history test and I didn't study."

Everyone relaxed. You couldn't die from a history test. Mom tried to stuff her with sliced banana.

"What's with you?" Jenny asked when Martha, out of habit, sat right down next to her on the school bus.

"Nothing," Martha said. She had no time even to be nasty to Jenny this morning. She couldn't wait to talk to Teddy.

"You're not having some kind of fit are you?" Jenny asked, watching Martha's knees knock together.

"I'm just cold," Martha said.

"You know what I think," Jenny said, and her big nose sniffed. "I think you caught the weirdos from your friend Teddy Winterrab."

"Oh, yeah?" Martha looked at Jenny. She rolled her eyes and stuck out her tongue. If Jenny thought she was having a fit of the weirdos, she would give her a good show.

"Gross!" Jenny said, and got up to change her seat. The bus driver yelled at her: "Siddown! No walking when the bus is moving." Jenny's face turned red.

Teddy was waiting at the doors, watching the buses again. This time Martha didn't try to sneak away.

"You should have warned me," she said. "You should have told me!"

Teddy just looked at her, and she realized it would take time to explain. But the first bell rang and that meant three minutes to class.

"Meet me for lunch," she said, and Teddy nodded.

It turned out there really was a history test. Martha had forgotten all about it. The sick feeling in her stomach got worse. She didn't even care if the Nose was whispering and snickering with Tessa and Diane. When the lunch bell rang, she grabbed her brown bag and flew to the cafeteria. Teddy was waiting at his back table, a pile of sandwiches spread out before him.

"Hey, Martha, I'm really glad," he said as she sat down.

"What about?"

"That you decided."

"What are you talking about?"

"You want to be my friend, right? You decided you don't care what people think."

Martha looked around the lunchroom. She had completely forgotten about feeling embarrassed to be seen talking to Windbag. It didn't seem to matter anymore.

She told him about the laundry room, Mellow Rollings, and Pinky.

"Now what do I do?" she asked. "How am I supposed to know what Pinky's message means? And what if she comes back? I mean, is it dangerous?"

Teddy was fidgeting with his banana and cheese sandwich, and he was turning a little green. Who wouldn't, eating such a horrible sandwich? He made choking sounds, and Martha got frightened, until she realized he was laughing.

"Forget it," she said. "You don't believe a word I said."

"I believe it, I believe it," Teddy protested, wiping his face with a paper napkin.

"Then why laugh?"

"That wasn't a ha-ha laugh," Teddy said. "It was a scared laugh."

"You're scared?"

He nodded.

"Terrific. You get me involved with dead spirits and then you get scared." But he looked so awful, she had to feel sorry. It looked like she really was turning out to be a medium. She might become a famous detective. Or get an A on the term exams. She'd be famous . . . on her own.

"Listen," she said to Teddy. "Don't worry. It was just a joke. I was kidding around."

Teddy shook his head.

"Thanks, Marth, but I know it's no joke."

"How?" she asked. Sometimes Teddy acted like the world's biggest know-it-all, as bad as Jemima.

"Because."

"Because *why?*"

"Because I know Pinky," he said. "I wish you had been kidding around, but there's no way you made up Pinky. I know she's real, because once I got a message from her."

"You did? Well, why do you look so sick?"

"To tell the truth, I liked *thinking* I believed in this stuff better than really *believing* in it."

Martha thought for a moment. "Yeah, I guess I know what you mean. It's fun to get scared, but you're kind of glad when it turns out to be a trick, like seeing a three-D horror movie."

"You know what, though?" Teddy asked.

"What?"

"It's a lot less scary with a friend."

Maybe, Martha thought. Maybe less scary. But a lot more complicated, especially when the friend was Teddy Windbag.

15.

A séance was needed, Teddy said. The two of them together would try to contact Pinky. "She's a little flaky," said Teddy, "so we need to combine forces." They needed privacy, with no adults snooping around. Saturday afternoon at Teddy's house was best because his mother would be away.

"Fine," Martha said, and remembered Mrs. Bender. Errrgg, she'd forgotten to tell Jemima about baby-sitting.

She waited for the best possible moment. You couldn't tell with Jemima, she was in a good mood one minute and a bad mood the next. Maybe she had a hot date with Larry Haggerty again.

"That jerk, are you kidding?" Jemima said when Martha brought it up. "I wouldn't give him the time of day."

But Jemima's face turned sad when she heard about baby-sitting. "What the heck, I can use the money," she said.

"You still do, don't you?" Martha asked.

"Do what?"

"Think he's the only reality."

"Who?" Jemima said, looking annoyed.

"Him."

"Who's him?"

"Lawrence A. Haggerty."

"For your information, I hate his guts," Jemima said, and threw a pillow.

Martha ducked. "What does the *A* stand for anyway? Awful?"

Jemima threw another pillow at her. "Get lost, fart-face."

Martha knew she was right. Jemima was still crazy about him.

When Mom came home, Jemima said, "I'm sitting for Harvey on Saturday afternoon," and Mom said, "Fine, but can you take Martha along? Dad and I won't be back from the Farleys' until late evening."

"This is ridiculous," Martha said. "I'm no baby. What's happening around here? One case of strep throat and I'm a prisoner for life."

Mom laughed, then got serious. "It's not that. It's this prowler still on the loose."

"I know how to lock a door," Martha grumbled.

"But the locks keep getting broken."

"Hey, wait a minute!" Martha shouted. "If this prowler is still on the loose, that means Mellow is innocent."

"Maybe," Mom said. "It's true that while he was at the police station, all the coin boxes in the laundry room were robbed. But a whole gang could be involved, and Mellow could be part of it."

"Well, you don't have to worry, I'm going to a friend's on Saturday."

"Oh, if you're going to Jenny's, that's all right," Mom said.

"Not Jenny!" Martha said. "Do you think she's the only person in the world who could be my friend? Anyway, she's not my friend, I told you. I don't have any friends anymore."

Mom looked puzzled. "Then where are you going on Saturday?"

This was getting complicated. What you needed was another word instead of *friend.* Something that meant a person you knew but not necessarily a friend. And it was a mistake to have argued. She should have let Mom believe it was Jenny. Now she wondered if she should lie and say Tessa or Diane. But in the state Mom was in, she might call up every hour on the hour.

"Teddy Winterrab," she admitted. When Mom looked blank, she added, "You know, the boy who brought my homework."

"Oh, him." Mom still looked vague. "I don't think I know his mother."

"She's very nice."

"I'll have to give her a call."

"What for?"

"Just to check, Martha! What on earth is the matter with you?"

"I know," Jemima said in a know-it-all way as she went to the kitchen.

"You don't know anything," Martha said. Sisters could not be considered friends. They were in a category by themselves.

Mom phoned just before dinner. As usual the adults ganged up on the kids. Teddy's mother might let him get away with murder, but she acted like a supernormal mother and said she could understand if Mrs. Lewis didn't approve of leaving the children unsupervised.

"You're right," Mom said to Martha when she'd hung up. "Teddy's mother is very nice. But she isn't going to be home on Saturday, so it's best if you go to the Benders."

"Teddy will be all alone," Martha said. "Maybe he should come to the Benders too."

"I don't think that's fair to either Mrs. Winterrab or Mrs. Bender," Dad said. "Do as your mother tells you, Martha."

Martha stared at her plate in a sulk. Jemima gave her a kick under the table, but Martha didn't respond.

"Don't pout," Dad said.

"I'm not," Martha said. "I'm being annoyed."

"I'm sure you can see Teddy another time," Mom said.

Jemima laughed and sprayed milk all over everyone. "Don't you guys see?" she crowed. "Martha's in love!"

Martha left the table and refused to help with the dishes. "I'm only a baby who can't stay home alone," she said. "Babies don't know anything about washing dishes."

She went to bed early. Before she turned out her light, she called to see if Pinky was lurking around. "If you're here, don't start throwing things around again, please," she said. "I want to get some sleep."

Nobody answered. Martha smacked her pillow and closed her eyes. Tomorrow Mrs. Gold would be sure to give a pop quiz on the spelling words she hadn't studied. Imagine trying to get Pinky to give her the answers to that. She would turn everything into a joke.

Suddenly the room seemed to grow cold. Martha sat up and looked to see if the window was open. It wasn't. Oh, no, she thought, I don't think I like this.

She pulled the covers over her head and scrunched her eyes closed. Maybe she could fall asleep before anything else happened.

But her ears were open and she heard the footsteps coming across the floor toward her bed. Dad walked by in the hall, whistling, and the footsteps stopped. Martha thought she was saved. But then they started again.

She didn't dare look, but she could imagine Pinky the ghost creeping toward her bed. Why had she ever gotten mixed up with dead people?

Martha hugged herself into a ball. Her feet felt like two icy-cold frogs. Maybe it won't know I'm here, she thought. And then the ghost's bony finger tapped her on the shoulder.

She didn't move, even though she felt like screaming. Another tap. And then a voice: "Marth?"

"Go away," Martha said in a shaky croak.

"Marth? I want to tell you something."

"I don't want to hear it! Get lost! Get out!"

"Well, shoot. That's the last time I do anything nice for you, kiddo."

Martha threw off the blankets and sat up. "Jemima? Hey, come back!"

Jemima stopped, then put her hand on her hip and gave one of her insulted looks, eyebrows up in her hair and mouth down to her navel.

"Sorry," Martha said. "I thought you were someone else."

"You were, like, expecting a visitor?"

"Must have been dreaming," Martha said. "Having a nightmare."

"Sure. Well, listen. All is not lost for your date on Saturday."

"My date?"

"What else? You can't fool me. You and your boyfriend, right?"

Before Martha could think of a protest, Jemima was rattling on.

"Of course, I can't exactly let you go to his house, but who's to complain if the boyfriend happens to ring the doorbell at the Benders? I mean, what's the harm with the big sister acting as a chaperon?"

Jemima did a little dance around the room. "Gosh" was all Martha could say. She could feel her eyes bugging out with the shock. When you least expected it, Jemima could act nice. Of course, she would ask for a favor in return, Martha knew. But for now it made things absolutely okay. And best of all, there was no ghost. Pinky had not been lurking around, and Martha felt positively warm with relief.

"Thanks," she said to Jemima.

"Think nothing of it," Jemima said, and turned to go. Then she stopped and hugged herself. "You know," she said, "it's freezing in here."

16.

The next morning Jenny sat next to her on the bus.
"I'm sorry about yesterday," she said.

Martha was surprised. A feeling of relief spread over her. Maybe she and Jenny would be friends again, and they could forget about Phyllis Blott. Anybody could make a mistake.

"I was only trying to help," Jenny said.

"Help?"

"You really shouldn't hang around with a person like that."

"You mean Teddy?"

"Who else would I be talking about?"

The relief vanished. Prickles of anger started on the top of Martha's head.

"It's none of your business who I hang out with," Martha said.

"I was only telling you as a friend . . ."

Martha looked at her. "You're not my friend. The Blot is your friend."

Jenny's eyes widened, and she began to sputter: "The Blot? Who . . ." And at that point Martha got up and changed her seat, and the bus driver didn't even yell.

Still, all through the morning she kept thinking that

maybe she was being unfair. Suppose Jenny was trying to be a real friend by worrying about her friendship with Teddy?

"And you, Martha?" Mrs. Gold was asking.

"Sorry. What?" Martha said. She hadn't been listening.

"Your composition. What topic will you write about?"

What composition? "Well, I haven't decided yet." Martha stalled. "Could I have until this afternoon?"

"You were supposed to have chosen a topic for homework, Martha," Mrs. Gold said. "But since you've been out sick so long, I think we can give you a little extra time."

"Thanks," Martha said, feeling crummy about getting special privileges. Everybody was glaring at her.

She would stop thinking about Jenny, Teddy, and Ouija boards and start concentrating on her schoolwork. Otherwise, her report card would be the pits.

I'm cracking down, she told herself, just as her dad would say when he made a resolution to do something. But Martha's resolution lasted only half an hour. Then the class went to the library to do research on their composition topics. Jenny, Tessa, Diane, and Phyllis Blott sat together at one of the tables. Instead of anger this time tears prickled behind Martha's eyes. Why did they all have to gang up on her?

She squinched her face into a frown so she wouldn't look pathetic or anything, and marched up to the librarian's desk.

"Can I help you with something?" Mr. Pumphrey asked.

"What have you got on ghosts?" Martha asked. That

would be a good topic for her composition. She had firsthand experience.

Mr. Pumphrey showed her the section. Martha took a stack of books and went to sit at a table by herself. She opened one of the books and tried to concentrate. But her teary eyes made the words go all blurry. It was a dumb book. It told about people who said they had seen ghosts, and then showed how the people were mistaken. The ghosts turned out to be shadows, or tricks or bad dreams. Martha took notes, but she didn't feel enthusiastic. Her glance kept wandering back to Jenny's table. The four of them were whispering together. Martha wondered if it was worth it. Was she going to have to choose between the Nose and the Blot, and Teddy Windbag?

She was surprised at lunchtime when Jenny said, "Come and sit with us, okay, Marth?"

At first Martha felt a little awkward, but in a couple of minutes it was like the old days before strep. It was nicer to be part of things. It felt good to be one of the gang. She unpacked her lunch and took a bite of her sandwich.

"We called this meeting," Jenny suddenly said, "because we've all been friends since kindergarten and that's a long time."

That was true for everybody except the Blot. She hadn't been in their kindergarten class, and she hadn't gone to summer day camp with them either.

"So we think we have a right to tell you what we want to say." Jenny's nose bobbed around the table and everybody nodded. "And I want to say that I think it's all sort of my fault. I shouldn't have sent that get-well card."

"Listen, that's okay," Martha started to say. She was surprised and sorry about what had happened. Probably she was at fault herself. Probably she had acted like a real nerd.

"Let me finish, will you?" Jenny snapped. "What I was saying was, I should have waited until you came back to school to tell you I was best friends with Phyllis. You were too sick to act normal about it."

"Huh?" Martha said.

"You know, it's a shock for sick people to get bad news," Phyllis Blott said, sticking out her vampire fangs in a hideous smile.

"Yeah," Tessa agreed. "It went straight to your brain and made you crazy."

"I'm not crazy," Martha said.

Jenny gave her a long look. "Well, if you're not, why are you still hanging around with that weirdo?"

"What weirdo?" Martha asked in the iciest tone she could manage.

"Oh, come on," they all groaned. "You know who we mean."

Martha began packing up her lunch. She didn't say anything because she couldn't think of something good enough.

The Nose, the Blot, and Tessa suddenly looked nervous. The Blot was picking the wax off her milk carton. Tessa was shredding her tinfoil, and the Nose was shifting from one foot to the other. Diane Fink didn't look nervous. She looked embarrassed. She was staring at the floor, her cheeks a funny orange color.

"So?" Jenny said.

"So." Martha took a breath. "So what I want to know is if any of you are interested in being friends with me."

Jenny stopped looking nervous and looked exasperated instead.

"Well, of course we do," she said. "That's the whole point of what I've been saying."

"I mean even if I hang around with Teddy."

Jenny gaped. "Well, why would you want to do that?"

"Why not?"

"It doesn't look good for us," Jenny said.

"It would kind of make us look like we were friends with him too," Tessa said.

Phyllis Blott nodded and picked wax out of her fingernails. Diane Fink didn't say anything; she still looked embarrassed.

Martha stared at them for a moment. "No, thanks," she said, and walked away.

"But, Martha!" Jenny wailed. "You can't."

"Why not?"

"Because. Because nobody's ever been friends with Teddy Windbag."

"I got news," Martha said. "Times have changed."

Jenny looked furious. "I'll tell you, Martha Lewis," she said, "you're not coming to my Halloween party this year! And don't think you can!"

"Who wants to?" Martha said, and went off across the lunchroom. She saw Teddy sitting at a table in the corner. She headed straight for it.

She'd forgotten about Halloween, though. Every year, after trick or treat, they had a party at Jenny's apartment, and Jenny's mother always had a special scary surprise for them. Martha hadn't really thought much about all the things she wouldn't be doing if she was no longer friends with Jenny.

As usual Teddy had his three sandwiches spread out.

"Hi," Martha said as she sat down.

"Hi," Teddy said, sounding cautious. He glanced over at Jenny's table. "What's been going on?"

"A discussion," Martha said, wanting to tell him about the Halloween party and how mad she was, as if it were his fault. She had to catch her breath. She couldn't start blaming things on Teddy. The only person you could blame for anything you did was yourself.

"We were talking about what to write for our class compositions," she told him. "I couldn't think of a topic before, but now I've got one."

"What is it?" Teddy asked.

"The meaning of friendship."

"Sounds pretty heavy."

"Nope, simple," Martha said. "I've got firsthand experience."

She looked at Teddy and he looked back at her, and she could tell by the way his eyes turned darker brown that he understood.

17.

Martha was working at the kitchen table when Dad came in.

"Homework?" he asked.

"I'm doing a report called 'What Is a Friend?' but I'm not sure I can figure it out," Martha replied. "It's awfully complicated."

"Being a friend can get complicated at times," Dad said. He got some fruit juice out of the refrigerator and poured himself a glass and one for Martha too.

"If a friend thinks you're doing something wrong, should the friend tell you?" Martha asked, chewing on her eraser.

Dad thought a moment. "There are people who think being a friend means giving advice," he said. "But sometimes our friends do things we don't agree with. The real test of friendship is letting the person go ahead and do those things, and then if it goes wrong, being there to help afterward."

Martha scribbled notes as Dad talked. Yes, she thought, that's what a really good friend would do. Jenny should let her be friends with Teddy even if it turned out to be a mistake.

"Don't forget, friendship is two-sided," Dad said.

"What you expect from your friends you have to be willing to give yourself."

He patted her head as he left the kitchen, but Martha just sat there, feeling as if she'd been hit with a wet sock. Two-sided meant that Martha had to let Jenny be friends with Phyllis Blott. Martha had all along been thinking about her own feelings and not Jenny's. In a way, they were in the same boat, she and Jenny. They both had new friends, and they both thought the new friends were wrong.

But how did you put all this stuff into a composition? Martha slaved at it for another hour. What is a friend? A friend is somebody who cares enough about you to let you do your own thing. And somebody who doesn't say "I told you so" when you fall flat on your face doing it.

Martha was glad she got the composition done. Now she would have Saturday free for the séance. After lunch she and Jemima walked over to the Benders'. Martha carried the Ouija board in the same old paper bag.

The Benders lived in Melody Woods in a private house. There were two big fat bushes of blue flowers in front and a lot of Harvey's toys strewn around the lawn.

"Harvey's taking a nap," Mrs. Bender said when she opened the door. She looked more like a movie star than ever. Mr. Bender came downstairs, and he looked like one too.

"Harvey will sleep for a couple of hours," Mrs. Bender told Jemima.

"Enjoy the peace and quiet while you can," Mr. Bender said, and winked.

No sooner had the Benders' car pulled out of the

driveway than the doorbell rang. It was Teddy. "I waited in the bushes until they left," he said.

Martha tried to ignore Jemima's smirks, and she and Teddy went down to the Benders' family room. Teddy drew the curtains even though the room was pretty shadowy, since it was in the basement.

"Do you think Jemima will barge in?" he asked.

"Nope. She'll be too busy talking on the phone."

They set up the board. Teddy had brought matches and a candle. When they lit it, eerie shadows crept up the walls and there was a funny smell. "It's my mother's," Teddy said, sniffing. "She likes cinnamon and cloves."

"I hope Pinky does too," Martha said, feeling a little scared all of a sudden. It was hard to believe that Pinky was a real ghost and they could talk to her.

"You call for her first," Teddy said. "And if she won't come, then I'll try." He got out a pad of paper and two sharp pencils.

Martha put her fingers on the planchette. It seemed to tremble a few times, but nothing happened. Martha knew Pinky wasn't around anyway, because the room stayed stuffy and warm.

"I'm getting a headache," she told Teddy. The candle smell was very strong. "What do we need that thing for?"

"Atmosphere," Teddy replied. He shut his eyes and rocked back and forth. "Pinky. Piiiinnnnkeeee?" he whispered.

Martha thought he was overdoing it.

Suddenly the door to the family room banged open.

"What's going on?" Jemima demanded, sniffing suspiciously. "And what are you guys doing down here in the dark?"

Martha couldn't think of any logical explanation. She hoped Teddy would say something, but he just sat there with his mouth open, looking surprised.

"It's just a board game," Martha said.

"Oh," Jemima said sarcastically. "And you had to light a candle because there's something wrong with the lights?" She flicked the switch, and an overhead fluorescent light glared. "Let me see that," Jemima said.

There was nothing else to do but confess. "We try to contact spirits," Martha explained, hoping it would sound like a silly kid's idea and Jemima would leave them alone.

But Jemima seemed interested.

"Did you ever make contact?" she asked.

"Not with that on," Teddy said, rolling his eyes to the ceiling.

To Martha's surprise, Jemima ran over and turned the light off. Then she hurried back to the Ouija board. "Come on, tell me, did you ever really talk to a spirit?"

"Nope," Martha said at the same time that Teddy said, "Sure."

Jemima looked from one to the other. "What happens then?" she asked.

"They tell you things by pointing to the letters on the board."

"What kind of things?"

"Anything. You ask them a question and sometimes they know the answer. Spirits know a lot of things that living people don't," Teddy said.

Jemima's eyes widened. "You mean you can really find things out? Like maybe what was in somebody else's mind?"

"Sometimes you only think you do," Martha said, remembering Teddy's advice about scientific notebooks.

"Move over," Jemima said. "I want to play too."

"What about Harvey?" Martha asked.

"It's okay, he's still asleep."

Jemima didn't know the rules. Instead of waiting for Pinky to appear, she just started rattling off questions. "Does he love me? Is he going to ask me to the dance next month?" Martha knew who she was talking about.

Pinky won't care about such dumb questions, she thought. The room stayed as warm as ever.

"See, I told you it doesn't work," Martha said.

"Come on, give it a chance," Teddy said. "Listen, Jemima, you're not doing it right. We have to make contact first. Let's all close our eyes and call for Pinky."

"We should hold hands," Jemima suggested, "like they do in horror movies."

"Somebody has to keep their fingers on the pusher," Martha said. She didn't fancy holding hands with Teddy, especially in front of Jemima.

They called for Pinky in quavery voices. Martha felt a little dopey. Now that Jemima was in on it, it wasn't so special anymore. In fact, Jemima made it seem like it was just a silly old game and nothing could possibly happen.

Suddenly the room grew cold.

Teddy said, "Here she comes."

Jemima looked around a little anxiously. The planchette began to move back and forth.

"Slow down, Pinky," Teddy said. "We just want to ask you a couple of questions."

"Does he love me?" Jemima broke in.

WHO? Pinky spelled.

110

"Eeerrr," Jemima said. "Uh, Larry Haggerty."

The plastic piece jumped up and down. *DON'T ASK ME,* it said. *ASK HIM.*

"But I can't," Jemima whined, just as if she were home having an argument with Mom. "You can't ask a boy a thing like that."

ASK HIM SOMETHING ELSE, Pinky said.

"Like what?" Jemima asked.

Martha felt annoyed. "Hey," she started to say. It wasn't fair for Jemima to hog the board.

But the planchette suddenly went still. It quivered slightly, almost as if it were thinking or listening to something. Then slowly it spelled out *VANILLA.*

"What's that supposed to mean?" Jemima asked.

WHAT HE WANTS, Pinky replied.

Jemima gave a snort of disgust and got to her feet.

YOUR LAST CHANCE. Pinky was spelling so fast that Teddy had trouble getting all the letters down. *VANILLA HURRY.*

"This is a really stupid game," Jemima said crossly. "And I was really stupid to get into it."

The plastic piece bounced up and down. *RED NAG,* it spelled.

"Pinky's mad," Teddy said. "After all, it's not a *game.*"

Jemima stomped out. Teddy let out a sigh of relief. "Now we can get down to business," he said. "Listen, Pinky, what we'd like to know is—"

A blood-curdling scream came from upstairs.

Martha dropped the planchette and Teddy dropped his pencil. They ran up to the kitchen.

"Kidnappers." Jemima was screeching. "Harvey's gone!"

18.

"It's probably not kidnappers," Martha said, unable to imagine anybody wanting to take Harvey anywhere. "He's probably wandering around."

But they looked all over the house and the yard and in the neighbors' yards. No Harvey.

"All because of that dumb game!" Jemima wailed.

"Well, what do we do now?" Martha thought aloud. They should call the police, she guessed. That's what you did when somebody was missing, in this case one child and a ratty gray pig.

Jemima blanched at the mention of police. "Oh, boy, am I ever gonna be in trouble," she said.

Martha could see how it would be a shame to get the police involved if Harvey had only taken a walk. "What we should do is ask Pinky," she said, but stopped when she saw Jemima's face.

"I never want to hear about that idiotic game again!" Jemima cried.

Teddy interrupted. "But I think Pinky tried to warn us. Look," he said, and showed them the pad he had used to take down Pinky's messages. "She told us 'vanilla hurry.' and 'red nag.' "

"What the heck does *red nag* mean?" Jemima said raising her eyebrows.

"It's an anagram," Teddy explained patiently. "When the letters of one word are mixed up to spell another. *Red nag* comes out *danger*. I don't think Pinky was answering your questions, Jemima. She was telling us about Harvey."

"Great," Jemima said. "But she didn't tell us much, did she? All she could say was *vanilla.*"

"I've got it!" Martha said. "It's all connected to the Morris ice cream store. First Pinky tells me to try Archie's wangle game. Of course, she spelled it 'A-r-c-h-e-e' but the message is clear. Now she's saying *vanilla*. How about vanilla ice cream? At least we can try. Maybe that's where Harvey went."

"It's true," Jemima said, a little awed. "Harvey loves vanilla cones with sprinkles, and Mrs. Bender always stops at Morris's."

The three of them tried to rush out of the door together. They raced down the street. Teddy was still holding on to his pad and pencil, and he was scribbling as he ran. Once he almost hit a lamppost, but Martha saved him.

"Another anagram!" he shouted as they crossed the wide street of traffic that separated Melody Woods from the shops and apartments. Jemima and Martha looked around anxiously. It was a relief that there were no ambulances or crowds. It meant Harvey had made it across.

"Listen," Teddy was saying. "That message about Archie's wangle game was an anagram too. Pinky doesn't have trouble with spelling."

"But how do we find out what it means?" Martha asked.

"I don't know. It's crazy. It must be a name because you were asking about the person in the laundry room. Aside from Archie, there could be a whole bunch of names in these letters. Charles, Nathan, Marc . . ."

"Try Mellow Rollings," Martha said.

Teddy shook his head. "No way." He went on scribbling. "Terry, Warren, gargle—"

"Gargle?"

"Sorry. Sam, Rawley, Larry . . ."

Martha stopped in her tracks, and Teddy and Jemima crashed into her.

"Larry?"

"Wait. I got a few more," Teddy said, but Martha stopped him.

"Try Larry Haggerty."

Teddy kept scribbling.

"Hey, you guys," Jemima said, but Teddy held up his hand dramatically.

"Yeah! I can get Haggerty. But not Larry too. And there are letters left over."

Martha thought a moment. "Try Lawrence Haggerty."

"Okay," Teddy said, "but there's still a few left. An *a*, an *m*, an *s*, and *e*."

"Ames," Jemima said slowly. "Lawrence Ames Haggerty. Why couldn't that dumb spirit give me the right answers if she knows his whole name?"

"It had nothing to do with your questions," Martha said soberly. It was too bad to disappoint Jemima, but there was a real possibility that Larry Haggerty was the one who had been breaking into the laundry room.

Jemima shook her head. "What we're supposed to be doing is finding Harvey," she said. "Come on."

Archie Morris was behind the counter when they arrived at the ice cream store.

"Hi, kids," he said. "What'll you have today? Want a taste of my Chocolate Chip Heaven? I made it to celebrate my luck. I'm going back to college in the spring."

"Wonderful," Martha said, "but we're looking for Harvey Bender. Have you seen him?"

Archie scratched his head.

Martha elaborated. "Little kid this high. His face is always screwed up like he's going to cry, and he carries a gross stuffed pig."

"Can't say for sure that I have," Archie said. "So many kids come in."

Explosions and outerspace laughter came from the video game at the back of the store. Jemima was staring at it like a person bewitched. Martha saw why. Larry Haggerty's overly long arms were at the controls. Clustered around him were five or six of his friends.

"Larry will help us," Jemima said, and went over to him.

Martha noticed the rude way he shrugged his shoulders when Jemima talked to him, as if she were a worm for interrupting. It would do Jemima good to find out the truth about Larry. But Martha felt a little afraid. She couldn't just go up and accuse him. He'd shrug her off, too, and tell her "Get lost, kid." She needed proof.

"Please, Larry, will you help us?" Jemima was saying. "If all you guys spread out, we could comb the neighborhood."

Larry just laughed. "Hey," he said. "Can't you see I'm busy?"

"I'm serious!" Jemima said, almost in tears.

"She's serious," Larry said in a high voice, and his friends cracked up. To them it was the biggest joke of the century.

Jemima's face was very red. She turned on her heel and bit her lip. Larry's big long arm came out and grabbed her. "Aw, come on," he said. "I was only fooling."

Jemima struggled. Larry pulled. Jemima gave him a push, and he grabbed her arm and got an ugly look on his face, worse than before. He wasn't fooling now.

"Hey!" Martha said, and without thinking, she ran right up to him and kicked him in the shins.

"You little rat!" Larry said, but Martha was fast. She quickly ran back the other way. Larry let go of Jemima and ran after her. Teddy pushed one of the iron ice cream store chairs in front of Larry, and Larry tripped. He and the chair fell together, hitting the floor with a thud.

Then there was the strange sound of things clinking and tinkling and rolling across the floor. Quarters. Hundreds of them!

It cost three quarters to do the wash and two quarters to dry it. Quarters were all that was in the money boxes in the laundry rooms at the Grape Hill Apartments. Quarters were what you used when you played video games.

Martha looked down and saw what she hadn't noticed before. Larry's feet were encased in blue-and-gray sneakers.

19.

Martha explained it all to Archie, and he agreed to call the police and tell them about Larry Haggerty. Larry had run out of the store, leaving all his quarters on the floor. He wouldn't do a thing like that if he wasn't guilty.

"But we should have told him to report Harvey too," Teddy protested as they left the ice cream store.

"Jemima's too scared to do that," Martha told him.

"If the police find out, the Benders will never ask me to baby-sit again!" Jemima cried.

"You won't have anyone to baby-sit for if we don't find Harvey," Teddy said ominously.

Jemima nodded. "You're right. This is too big for us to handle alone."

"We just nabbed the laundry room prowler alone," Martha said. "I'm sure we can find a little kid and a grungy pig."

"Let's start searching, then," Teddy said. "Where first?"

Martha thought a moment. "I say we go back and ask Pinky."

Jemima moaned and Teddy looked disgusted. "Get serious, Martha," he shouted. "This is no time to fool around."

"What do you mean, fool around?" Martha shouted back.

"Asking Pinky! We need to take direct action. Harvey could get run over or really get kidnapped if we wait too long."

"Yeah, we have no time for silly games, Martha," Jemima said in a tone like a teacher.

They were ganging up on her. "But Pinky did warn us about Harvey," she said. "And she gave me the clue to Larry Haggerty. She could help now."

Teddy looked doubtful. "This is different. We have to be sensible."

"I suppose a Ouija board is not sensible?" Martha asked. "You're the one who suggested it in the first place, if you remember."

Teddy kicked at the ground with his heel. "I know."

"And you're the one who wanted me to be your friend!"

"I said when you were ready," Teddy said.

Martha glared at him. "If losing all my other friends just to be friends with you doesn't mean I'm ready, I don't know what does! Are you telling me we're *not* friends?"

"No, no," Teddy said. "We're friends, we're friends."

Martha nodded. "So if you're my friend, the least you could do is agree with me."

"Uh-uh," Teddy said, shaking his head. "Being friends doesn't mean you have to agree with them all the time. We can agree to disagree and still be friends."

That's what her dad had said. But Martha didn't want to think about that now. She felt sure Pinky would help, and she'd like it a lot better if Teddy agreed with her.

"I hate to remind you two, but we have a little problem?" Jemima said. "While you've been having your big discussion, I've been thinking. I know I'm in big trouble, but we better go to the police."

Jemima suddenly looked very grown-up and sensible. Maybe it was because she had had to face facts about Larry.

"I guess you're right," Martha said, and Teddy nodded.

They were right across from the Grape Hill police station when somebody called from a distance. Two familiar figures were coming down the street, holding hands. One was Mellow Rollings. The other was a little kid dragging a stuffed pig and licking an ice cream bar.

"Harvey!" Jemima screamed. Her face broke into a gigantic smile. Then she scowled. "You little dip! Where have you been?"

Harvey looked up at her. His nose was running, and there was ice cream all over his face. "Vanilla," he said.

Mellow was staring at Jemima but trying to look like he wasn't.

"Hi, guys," he said. "You know this kid?"

"Know him!" Jemima cried. "I'm going to murder him!"

"What are you doing with Harvey?" Martha asked.

But Mellow didn't pay any attention to her. He only had eyes for Jemima. His voice cracked when he spoke, and he had to clear his throat.

"The kid told me he woke up and nobody was home. So he went to find a baby-sitter. I guess that means you, Jemima."

Jemima smiled at him, and Mellow blinked. "I was, er,

hanging out and the kid came along and looked lost. I couldn't get a straight answer about who he was or where he lived, but he sure did want an ice cream. I got him one at the Good Humor, then I figured I better take him to the police station."

"Oh, Harvey," Jemima said, and sat down on the sidewalk and gave the boy a hug. Harvey mushed vanilla ice cream into her hair.

"So where did you find him exactly?" Teddy asked.

"Uh," Mellow said. "Er. Around near the apartments. Smart kid. He knew where you lived Jemima." As soon as Mellow said it he clamped his jaws shut.

"What were you doing around the apartments," Martha asked. "You don't live there, do you?"

Mellow jumped as if he'd been stuck with a poker. "Oh, no! I was hanging out, that's all."

"Just hanging out," Martha mumbled. "Not by the laundry room by any chance?" She hoped it wouldn't turn out that Mellow was one of the laundry room gang. She was going to ask him a few more questions when Teddy jabbed her in the ribs.

"Shut up," he whispered. "Don't you see?"

"Gosh," Jemima was saying, still smiling at Mellow and hugging Harvey. "I'm so glad you were there."

They looked into each other's eyes and laughed. Mellow put out his hands and helped Jemima to her feet.

Martha sighed. Yeah, sure, she understood now. Mellow had been hanging out, hoping to catch a glimpse of Jemima. A lucky thing for all of them. Jemima had a replacement for Larry Haggerty. Mellow's arms were the proper length, and he was almost cute. In fact, a lot cuter than Larry Haggerty.

"All's well that ends well," Teddy proclaimed in his official voice. He looked at Martha. "That's from a play."

"I know," she said, and gave him a jab to pay him back.

They were walking toward Melody Woods when they saw Diane Fink on her bicycle. She called to them.

"I'm so glad I met you," she said excitedly. "I have something here." She fished around in her knapsack and came up with two envelopes. "I didn't know your address, Ted," she said, handing him one. She gave the other to Martha. "They're invitations," she explained. "To my Halloween party."

Teddy looked at his as if it were the first invitation he'd ever received. Maybe it was.

Martha stammered, "But isn't Jenny having her party this year?"

Diane shrugged. "I got to thinking about what Jenny said to you the other day. I personally don't care if you're friends with Teddy Windbag or the man in the moon! Sorry, Ted. Anyway, I decided to start my own group of friends."

"I accept your invitation," Teddy said very formally. "Thank you very much, Diane."

"Me too," Martha said. She had a funny feeling in her chest. She didn't know what it was. It felt a little like happiness, and a little like sadness.

"I'm sort of nervous," Diane admitted. "Jenny always had these great parties. I don't know if I can think up anything even half as good. My mom isn't much help either."

"I could make a suggestion," Teddy said. "But it could get pretty spooky."

"The spookier the better!" Diane said. "What is it?"

Teddy gave Martha a look. "A surprise," he said. "What do you think, Marth? Halloween is a good time for ghosts. Should we help out?"

Martha smiled. "Sure," she said, understanding that the feeling in her heart was getting happier by the minute. "After all, what are friends for?"

Masterful mysteries
by
PHYLLIS REYNOLDS NAYLOR

> **Winner of the Edgar Allan Poe Award**

☐ **NIGHT CRY**   40017-1 $2.95
Scaredy-cat Ellen Stump <u>really</u> has something
to worry about when a suspicious stranger
starts hanging around her house just after a
local boy is kidnapped

☐ **THE WITCH HERSELF**   40044-9 $2.95
Lynn and her best friend Mouse are terrified
when Lynn's mother sets up an office in the
home of a dangerous witch!

☐ **THE WITCH'S SISTER**   40028-7 $2.95
Lynn is convinced her sister, Judith, is a witch–
especially after she sees her conjure up a real
live boy from the middle of a lake!

☐ **WITCH WATER**   40038-4 $2.95
Lynn and Mouse are off on another
witch hunt—only this time it's a spooky
old neighbor that they're after...

Wonderful Family Stories
for Young Readers

BETSY
BYARS